"I am not on the prowl for a sugar daddy!"

Claudia said, bolting to her feet.

Hayden shot her a wry look. "I'm not old enough for that!"

Claudia tried to clamp down on her rising temper. Which, in itself, was a new task for her. She wasn't a woman who let herself get angry about anything. Until now. But there was something about this powerful, compelling man that drove her crazy—and they'd only just met!

"The only—and let me repeat, the *only*—reason I'm here is because I tracked you through your boat's registration."

His expression suddenly wary, he stepped toward her. "Are you digging into my personal affairs? Because if you are, I'll personally toss you out of here."

"I'm here because—" She sucked in a fierce breath, then heaved out the next words. "Because you're the man I—I can't get out of my mind."

Dear Reader,

With summer nearly here, it's time to stock up on essentials such as sunblock, sandles and plenty of Silhouette Romance novels! Here's our checklist of page-turners to keep your days sizzling!

❑ *A Princess in Waiting* by Carol Grace (SR #1588)—In this ROYALLY WED: THE MISSING HEIR title, dashing Charles Rodin saves the day by marrying his brother's pregnant ex-wife!

❑ *Because of the Ring* by Stella Bagwell (SR #1589)—With this magical SOULMATES title, her grandmother's ring leads Claudia Westfield to the man of her dreams....

❑ *A Date with a Billionaire* by Julianna Morris (SR #1590)— Bethany Cox refused her prize—a date with the charitable Kane O'Rourke—but how can she get a gorgeous billionaire to take no for an answer? And does she really want to...?

❑ *The Marriage Clause* by Karen Rose Smith (SR #1591)— In this VIRGIN BRIDES installment, innocent Gina Foster agrees to a marriage of convenience with the wickedly handsome Clay McCormick, only to be swept into a world of passion.

❑ *The Man with the Money* by Arlene James (SR #1592)— A millionaire playboy in disguise romances a lovely foster mom. But will the truth destroy his chance at true love?

❑ *The 15 lb. Matchmaker* by Jill Limber (SR #1593)— Griff Price is the ultimate lone cowboy—until he's saddled with a baby and a jilted-bride-turned-nanny.

Be sure to come back next month for our list of great summer stories.

Happy reading!

Mary-Theresa Hussey
Senior Editor

Please address questions and book requests to:
Silhouette Reader Service
U.S.: 3010 Walden Ave., P.O. Box 1325, Buffalo, NY 14269
Canadian: P.O. Box 609, Fort Erie, Ont. L2A 5X3

Because of the Ring

STELLA BAGWELL

SILHOUETTE *Romance*®

Published by Silhouette Books

America's Publisher of Contemporary Romance

For two real heroes,
Kenneth Finster and Billy Wilson.
With much appreciation and many thanks.

SILHOUETTE BOOKS

ISBN 0-373-19589-3

BECAUSE OF THE RING

Copyright © 2002 by Stella Bagwell

This edition published by arrangement with Harlequin Books S.A.

® and TM are trademarks of Harlequin Books S.A., used under license. Trademarks indicated with ® are registered in the United States Patent and Trademark Office, the Canadian Trade Marks Office and in other countries.

Visit Silhouette at www.eHarlequin.com

Printed in U.S.A.

Books by Stella Bagwell

STELLA BAGWELL

sold her first book to Silhouette in 1985. More than forty novels later, she still loves her job and she says she isn't completely content unless she's writing. Recently she and her husband of thirty years moved from the hills of Oklahoma to Seadrift, Texas, a sleepy little fishing town located on the coastal bend. Stella says the water, the tropical climate and the seabirds make it a lovely place to let her imagination soar and to put the stories in her head down on paper.

She and her husband have one son, Jason, who lives and teaches high school math in nearby Port Lavaca.

Dear Reader,

Last spring my husband and I were invited by our county commissioner to join him on a trip to Matagorda Island, a forty-mile strip of land that lies off the coast of Texas and which was once the location of an army air base during WWII and for many years afterward.

Although most of the barracks and military buildings have been dismantled or washed away by Hurricane Carla and the island is inhabited only by a few Texas Parks and Wildlife rangers, the flat landscape is still crisscrossed with concrete runways and landing strips. As I stood on one such strip, I was instantly overwhelmed with the history around me, and my writer's imagination took flight. The airmen who'd been stationed there to serve our country must have had lovers, wives, families. Did some of them go to war and never return?

I told myself that someday I would write about such an airman on Matagorda Island, and the chance came sooner than I expected when my editor invited me to do a book for the SOULMATES project.

Because of the Ring is more than just a story about a magical ring handed down from one generation to the next. It's about a love so powerful it can transcend all time and distance and bring two troubled hearts together in the most unexplainable and wondrous way.

I hope you enjoy Claudia and Hayden's mystical journey and, like them, I hope each of you is blessed with the magic of love.

Love and God bless,

Chapter One

Claudia Westfield managed to slide into the seat of her car without spilling hot coffee down the front of her dress or dropping the stack of books and papers jammed beneath one arm.

Even though it was only six-thirty, she wanted to arrive at work early. Exams for the final semester were concluding this week and she had a scad of papers to grade and scores to register and average.

The motor was running and she was reaching to pull the gearshift into Reverse when a wave of dizziness suddenly sent her head spinning.

Alarmed, especially when she'd never been sick a day in her adult life, Claudia gently leaned her head back against the seat and closed her eyes. Hopefully, a few moments of quiet would straighten her equilibrium.

The next thing she knew a man's face appeared against the canvas of her closed eyelids. The image was sharp and focused and so very real, she unconsciously gasped out loud.

Stunned by the unearthly sight, Claudia's eyes popped open and she glanced wildly around her. The driveway leading up to her apartment and the small manicured lawns of her bordering neighbors looked normal. Yet she could still see the man in her peripheral vision. He had dark wavy hair and cobalt-blue eyes that seemed to be peering straight at her. A somewhat sexy smile twisted his lips and exposed bright white teeth against dark skin.

"Oh. No. No," she whispered the denial. "This is— you're not really there. I'm just tired. Too tired."

Frantically she snatched the coffee cup from its holder on the dash and gulped at the still-hot liquid. The drink scalded her tongue, but she didn't care. The feeling was real and normal.

More careful now, she took a second sip and then a third. After that she dared herself to look out the windshield again. Thankfully, the man was gone and everything was as it should be.

She allowed herself to breathe again. Then slowly she closed her eyes to make sure he'd disappeared from that aspect of her vision, too. Relief washed through her. The man with the smiling face had disappeared.

Deciding there was nothing to panic about, she put the car into Reverse and backed onto the street. But moments later as she headed into the already busy Fort Worth traffic, she realized her hands were slick with sweat and she was trembling from head to toe.

You're cracking up, Claudia. Really and truly cracking up.

By lunchtime Claudia had more or less put the incident of the vision out of her mind. At least she thought she had until she met up with her friend, Liz, in the school cafeteria.

Secretary to one of the assistant principals, the high-spirited redhead who was slightly older than Claudia was the exact opposite of her quiet nature. Even so, they'd been pals from the first day they'd met two years ago.

Now as the women inched through the serving line, Liz's worried stare had Claudia clutching an unwitting hand to her throat.

"What in heck is wrong with you?" she asked.

"Me? Nothing. Why?"

Liz said, "You look like the bride of Frankenstein right after she was shocked to life."

Trying her best to joke away Liz's concern, Claudia touched a hand to her smooth brown hair. "Why? Have I suddenly developed two gray streaks?"

"No. You look totally drained."

"That shouldn't be surprising. This is finals week, Liz. Where have you been?"

"Don't play cute with me. This job never gets you down. Although, I don't know why. If I had to deal with some of the lazy, insubordinate students that come through Judith's office, I'd throw my hands up and scream. You, on the other hand, have a knack for bringing out the better side of these kids."

After exiting the serving line the two women took a seat at a vacant table. Immediately, Liz dug into her plate of chicken pot pie, but as soon as she realized Claudia was ignoring her food, she looked up in silent question.

"Something happened to me this morning, Liz," Claudia announced with grim resolve. "I think I'm going crazy."

Liz chuckled. "Aren't we all."

Urgently, Claudia leaned forward and lowered her voice. "No. I mean, really crazy. Like delusional. I think…I need to make a doctor's appointment for a checkup."

Hearing the concern in her friend's voice, Liz frowned. "Why? What happened?"

"I had visions of a man."

Liz didn't just chuckle this time, she outright laughed. "I'd be more worried if you weren't having visions of a man," she finally managed to say.

Frustrated, Claudia picked up her fork and jabbed at the lump of meat loaf on her plate. "I'm not talking about having a fantasy of the opposite sex, Liz. This was something totally different. This was a sharp, clear image that came to me out of the blue. No...it wasn't exactly out of the blue. I got dizzy first and then—" A trembling deep inside her made it difficult to go on. She gripped the fork and tried to breathe normally. "This face appeared."

"Aha! You got dizzy," Liz repeated with confidence. "See, there's a physical reason for this. And I'd say it was stress. Or it could be hormonal. Maybe your body is trying to tell you that you need a mate." She studied Claudia with renewed thoughtfulness. "Did you recognize this man?"

"No."

"Hmm. How strange. Was he nice?"

Claudia forked a piece of meat loaf to her mouth and chewed automatically. She didn't want to think about the man. Or the incident. The whole thing had been completely out of the ordinary and totally frightening.

"What do you mean by 'nice'? I'm not so far gone that I tried to talk to the man, Liz!"

Her friend waved an impatient hand at her. "I meant was his image appealing or did you get the feeling he was not someone you'd want lurking around you?"

Claudia's head tilted to one side as she considered Liz's question. "I was too stunned to think much. But I guess he was…nice. Not evil." She shook her head and groaned with disbelief. "What am I doing? I'm a science teacher! My job is to teach students about logical reasons. For instance, the shamrock is green because of chlorophyll, not because some Irish elf painted it that way. A rainbow is created by refraction and reflection of sunlight in raindrops. It's not some magical guide to a pot of gold. And a vision—well, there's always an explanation for them, too."

"Well, I'll be hanged," Liz said with exaggerated disappointment. "I guess I must have had too many absent days in science class. Here I've been chasing after rainbows, believing I was going to find some gold at one end."

"This isn't funny," Claudia snapped.

Claudia's testiness caused the other woman's brows to arch. "I wasn't trying to be funny. In fact, I feel sorry for you, Claudia."

Claudia's mouth gaped open. Sympathy was the last thing she expected from Liz. "Sorry! I don't want that, either! I want—" She made a frustrated gesture with her hand. "I want explanations!"

Liz popped a cherry tomato into her mouth and chewed with pleasure before she replied, "Look, Claudia, one of these days you're going to learn that there are mystical, magical powers at work in our lives. And they're something that can't be analyzed or reasoned out in a science lab."

Claudia huffed out a breath. "Well, you believe what you want. As for me, I'm sticking to my science lab. Or a doctor's office!"

A week later Claudia walked out of the doctor's office and headed home without a prescription or a concrete explanation for the vision she'd had or the ones that had subsequently followed these past few days.

Physically there was nothing ailing her, the doctor had assured her. He'd went on to suggest that she take a long vacation to rest her mind from the stress of her job and later, if the visions continued, she could always make an appointment with a psychiatrist.

A psychiatrist! Was she really becoming that emotionally unhinged? There wasn't any reason for it! She was an average young woman with a normal life, she reasoned with herself. Except that she spent odd times out of the day looking at a man she'd never seen in her life. And to make matters worse, the images were growing more detailed. The man appeared to be wearing some sort of uniform with a tie. Several times she'd pictured a stretch of water and a boat. There had also been a big white house with a widow's walk. None of it seemed to tie together or to make any sense.

Inside her apartment, she went straight to her computer and logged on to the Internet. She was going to take her doctor's advice and buy plane tickets to Cancun. A few days' rest might be exactly what she needed.

A few days with a man is what you need, Claudia.

The words zinged through her head so quickly she didn't know where they came from. But the suggestion sounded suspiciously like something her grandmother would have said to her.

Dear Lord, was she starting to hear voices now along with seeing things? she wondered wildly.

Shaking her head, she glanced down at her hands resting on the keyboard. Betty Fay's opal ring was still there on her hand and for long moments Claudia studied the piece of jewelry as though it was a piece of bacteria on a microscopic slide. At one time she'd believed the ring had led her to Anthony. She'd believed it so strongly that she'd refused to give up on their rocky relationship. It had taken proof of his infidelity to finally make her see the light. But by then she'd already endured a great deal of pain and humiliation.

Claudia would be a fool to think the ring had anything to do with her visions. To even consider it would be admitting that she still believed the piece of jewelry carried some sort of magical power. And she didn't believe in such things! It was pure hogwash!

But the first vision occurred the morning after she'd starting wearing the ring again, she argued with herself. What would happen if she took it off? Maybe that would fix her problem. Not a vacation in Cancun!

A week later Claudia smiled happily at Liz. "I'm fixed! I'm cured. No more visions."

"I wondered why you sounded so chipper when you picked up the phone this morning. And I didn't have to do much begging to get you to come over for a swim."

The two women had already made a few laps around the in-ground pool in Liz's backyard. They were now stretched out in lounge chairs and sipping iced lemonade.

"You can't imagine what a relief it is to know you're not losing your sanity, Liz. I wasn't relishing the idea of getting on a psychiatrist's couch."

"So what happened?" Liz asked. "How do you know you're cured?"

The hot sun was seeping into Claudia's muscles, relaxing them from the workout in the cool water. For the first time in days she felt like a whole person again. "Because I haven't seen *him* anymore. Not since I took off Gran's ring and that's been a week ago. Before, I was seeing him on a daily basis."

Frowning, Liz sat up and swung her legs over the side of the lounge. "You mean to tell me that taking off a ring stopped your visions? That's hard to swallow. Even from somebody who chases after rainbows."

"I'd be the first one to admit it sounds farfetched, but I can't dispute the facts. No ring, no visions," Claudia told her.

"Hmm. Could be coincidental."

Now it was Claudia's turn to frown. "What is this? You sound like you don't want me to be cured."

"It's not that. I'm just wondering—aren't you the teeniest bit curious as to why this ring makes you see things? Looks to me like you're just avoiding the problem. Not curing it."

Claudia groaned loudly. "Oh, brother! Why should a person go around asking for trouble? School has just ended. I have the summer ahead to relax. I don't want to spend it having some strange man pop up in my vision at any given moment."

"It was only two weeks ago that you were telling me that as a science teacher you liked to have reasons and explanations. Well? Don't you want them now?"

Claudia glanced at the pool of cool, glittering water. "No. I—I'm perfectly content to let things be. The visions were…" She swallowed and glanced back at her friend. "Frankly, they were too disturbing, Liz. There was something—oh, I don't know—*intimate* about the whole thing. I kept getting the feeling that this man knows me. In here." She tapped the middle of her chest, then shook her head. "It was eerie. I—I've decided the best thing for me to do is to get rid of the ring. So far it's brought nothing but misery to my life."

Liz gasped. "Oh, no, Claudia! It's a precious memento of your grandmother's. Besides, without it you might never figure out any of this."

"Figure it out?" Claudia repeated in disbelief. "I just want to forget it!"

"Coward!"

"I'm not!"

"Prove it," Liz dared.

San Antonio. It wasn't exactly Cancun, but for now Claudia considered it as a first step on her quest to find the man who'd been plaguing her waking hours ever since she'd returned the opal to her finger.

From her third-floor hotel room, she stared down at the Paseo del Rio winding its way through the city. Eighty-degree weather was mild for early June in south Texas and Claudia wished she could enjoy it with a boat ride or a drink at one of the outside cafés on the river walk. She wished she could do anything besides meet with a man she'd never laid eyes on. Especially when she had no idea how to explain the reasons that had prompted her to make this search. But she hadn't come to San Antonio on a pleasure trip and the sooner she got this job over with, the better she would feel.

Claudia found the office building in the old downtown part of the city a few blocks away from the famous Alamo. Mr. Hayden Bedford. He owned a roustabout company and from what she gathered from the plush complex of offices, a very profitable one. But then, most businesses that had anything to do with the oil field were money-makers. With the right man at the helm, she corrected herself.

Apparently Mr. Bedford knew his business. He just didn't know Claudia Westfield. And from the tone of his secretary when Claudia had called to schedule a meeting, he didn't want to know her. But somehow she'd managed to convince the older woman to give her an appointment anyway.

Now that the time was here, Claudia realized her mouth was dry and her heart was thud, thud, thudding at an unhealthy speed. Which was totally out of character. She wasn't a nervous person. Until now. And the suspicious, almost dour looks Mr. Bedford's secretary was throwing her way didn't help matters.

Damn it, Gran. This ring of yours is ruining me!

"All right, Ms. Westfield. Mr. Bedford can see you now."

Rising from her seat, Claudia brushed at the wrinkles in her skirt then headed toward a wooden door with a gold nameplate attached at eye level.

After knocking lightly, she stepped inside.

"Just a moment. I've got to get this damn light off my desk."

The deep male voice was coming from a man standing at the window, his back to her. At the moment he was adjusting the blinds so that the glaring afternoon sun tilted toward the ceiling rather than at him and the massive oak desk.

Claudia stood in the middle of the room, waiting for him to turn around. As the seconds ticked by she noticed he was dressed as a rancher rather than a businessman. Starched jeans. White tailored shirt, sleeves rolled back against his forearms. A dark leather belt studded with Texas lone stars. His dark wavy hair told her he was still young and his big, muscular body told her that he didn't always sit behind a desk.

"There. That's better," he said, then turned to face her.

Claudia stared and wondered if she was going to faint. Her knees were turning to sponges and there was a faint buzzing in her ears.

"You!" she said weakly.

Baffled by her reaction, he stepped around the desk, all the while keeping a careful eye on her pale face. "I'm Hayden Bedford," he introduced himself. "Are you Ms. Westfield?"

She nodded and attempted to lick her dry lips. "Yes. Yes, I am," she said, then offered him her hand. "I'm sorry. I'm sure I must look like a fool, but I...wasn't expecting to recognize you."

He took her hand in his, but rather than shake it, he simply held it firmly as his gaze scanned her face.

Hysteria rose up in Claudia as heat seemed to arc from his fingers to hers. Those were the same blue eyes, she thought frantically. The same square jaw and chin, the same hollow cheeks. Seeing her vision in the flesh was incredible—and terrifying.

"I think I should be the one to apologize," he said. "Because I can't say that I remember meeting you."

Hearing his voice seemed to help her pull herself together. Hoping she appeared far more normal than she felt, she said, "You haven't."

The marginal widening of his eyes had her quickly adding, "I mean...I'm pretty sure we've never met before."

"Are you feeling up to this interview, Ms. Westfield? You look a little pale."

In fact, Hayden was fairly certain he'd seen dead people with more color in their cheeks. But in spite of her paleness, she was an attractive woman. A little plain to suit his taste, but then, she wasn't here to supply him with female diversion, he reminded himself.

She was dressed in a white linen sheath and her light brown hair was pulled back at her nape and fastened with a white clasp. Her eyes were a soft brown and her skin was tanned. And suddenly he had the image of biting into a warm, golden marshmallow.

"I'm...I'll be all right," she replied. "And I'll try not to take up too much of your time, Mr. Bedford. Thank you for agreeing to see me on such short notice."

Still holding her hand, he cupped her elbow with his free hand and led her over to a leather chair that was angled toward the front of his desk.

"There now," he said as she sank onto the cushion. "Why don't you go ahead and tell me what it is you wanted to see me about. It's pretty obvious you're not here to contract a roustabout crew."

She tried to swallow, but her throat was so dry it refused to work. "No. I don't dabble in oil or gas wells, Mr. Bedford. I'm here because—I'm looking for a man."

Surprise flickered across his face. Then folding his arms across his chest, he shot her an amused smile. "There aren't any available men where you come from, Ms. Westfield?"

Claudia was so rattled it took her a moment to digest his meaning. When it did finally register, her spine stiffened to a prim line. Her chin jutted forward. "Fort Worth has plenty of men. I'm looking for one certain one."

Still amused, he said, "Hmm. I'm intrigued that your search brought you here. I wasn't aware that I'd made any bachelor lists."

Somehow his arrogance angered her enough to get her shocked juices going again. Color blossomed in her face and her eyes darkened. "I'm not aware of it, either, Mr.

Bedford," she said in a clipped tone. "In fact, I know nothing about your marital status. I found you because of a number. Or maybe I should say, a number on a boat."

A puzzled frown pulled his dark brows together and Claudia realized that, as the man in her vision, this man was by no means handsome, yet there was a rough masculinity about his craggy face and sinewy body that made his appearance totally unforgettable.

"I've got to admit I've had some odd encounters with women over the years. But I've never had one go to this length to meet me."

She silently groaned with impatience. "I'm not here to meet you, Mr. Bedford!"

"You're not here to hire roustabout services and you're not here to meet me. If that's the case, then it looks as though you're taking up my valuable time, Ms. Westfield."

She bolted to her feet. "And frankly, Mr. Bedford, your assumptions are downright insulting! For your information, I'm not on the prowl for a sugar daddy!"

He shot her a wry look. "I'm not old enough to be your sugar daddy."

Claudia's nostrils flared as she breathed deeply and tried to clamp a hold on her rising temper. Which in itself was a new task for her. She wasn't a woman who let herself get angry about anything. Until now.

"I don't care how old you are, mister!" She pushed the words through gritted teeth. "The only—and let me repeat—the *only* reason I'm here is because your name and address matches the number on the boat registration."

Her outburst seemed to get through to him and his

eyes narrowed as he studied her with new regard. "What boat are you talking about?"

She slashed a hand through the air. "I'm not sure what kind of boat it is. Except that it has sails and I think the name written on the bow was something like *Stardust* or *Skydust*."

"*Stardust*," he informed her. "And what has my boat got to do with you? She's not for sale."

Claudia met his cool blue gaze and tried not to shiver from the contact. "I'm not interested in buying your boat. It just happened to be the only clue I had to start with."

His expression suddenly wary, he stepped toward her. "Start what? Digging into my personal affairs? Are you with some insurance company? Because if you are, I'll personally toss your little butt right out of here."

To her horror, her hand was suddenly itching to slap his face. She, a person who wouldn't even step on a spider, wanted to inflict bodily pain on another human being! This man was doing something to her and whatever it was had to be bad.

"I am not with any sort of insurance company. I'm a high school science teacher and I'm here because—" She sucked in a fierce breath, then heaved out the next words. "Because you're the man I—I can't get out of my mind!"

Chapter Two

The man had the nerve to laugh.

"Oh, honey, come on, you got some mixed signals somewhere. I never did think I was God's gift to women. And you shouldn't, either. In fact, the opposite sex seems to want to take me in small doses. You probably will, too."

"I can certainly see why," Claudia intoned, then stomped toward the door.

Suddenly he was blocking her path and she teetered back on her heels to keep from plowing into him.

"Where are you going?"

Her jaw rigid, she folded her arms across her breasts. "Goodbye, Mr. Bedford. I can't really say it's been a pleasure meeting you."

His head swung back and forth in a menacing way and Claudia found her gaze sliding from his thick shoulders and wide chest to his long, muscular legs. She'd been around strong, athletic men before, but this man was different. There was something blatantly masculine about him. Something that made her think of procreation rather than recreation.

Dear heaven, it was time she got out of here, Claudia thought. The last thing she needed was to add sexual fantasies to her visions of the man.

"No," he corrected in a voice too smooth to be nice. "You're not going anywhere just yet. We haven't gotten this matter straightened out."

She arched a haughty brow at him. "There is no matter. I—I found what I was looking for. And that's the end to it."

Wrinkles furrowed his forehead. "You wanted to find me and now that you have, that's it? You're going to leave?"

"That's about the size of it."

"Just a minute," he muttered, then opening the door, he said to his secretary, "Hold all my calls, Lottie, and radio Vince to let him know I'll be late getting out to the site."

Claudia stood her ground and tried to gather herself together as she waited for him to shut the door. When he finally turned back to her, she said, "I think it's you who are wasting my time now, Mr. Bedford. I have no intentions of discussing anything else with you! You're arrogant and assuming and—"

His features tight, he took her by the arm and this time led her to a long leather couch positioned against one wall of the office.

"You're the one who made an appointment to see me," he reminded her as she sat. "And you're the one who barged in here and started spouting nonsense."

"'Nonsense'!" she echoed with outrage, then jumped to her feet.

Immediately, he caught her by the shoulder and pushed her back down to the couch.

"Stay put!"

Claudia bounced right back up in his face. "Don't tell me what to do. I'm leaving! Now step out of my way!"

Ruefully he shook his head. "I didn't want to have to do this," he told her. "But it looks like I don't have any other choice."

Air whooshed from her lungs as she suddenly found herself flattened against his hard chest.

"What—"

The question was literally smothered beneath his lips. Unprepared for such an intimate onslaught, she stood paralyzed. Then her mind began to spin and she felt herself going hot and cold, then hot again.

Her hands formed two fists and she raised them to whack at his shoulders, but they never reached their destinations. Before she could fight back, he pulled his mouth away from hers and grinned down at her.

"Feel better now?"

He needed his foot stomped, but she realized she just didn't have the strength to do it. Kissing this man had left her weak and quivering.

"I've never been so insulted in my life!"

"Sorry, I'm out of practice." He lowered his mouth toward hers. "Maybe I should try again."

Ducking away from him, Claudia collapsed onto the couch and gulped in several breaths of air. "You'll do nothing of the sort!"

He'd been wrong a few moments ago, Hayden realized as he looked down at her. She wasn't a plain woman. Now that he'd kissed her, every nuance of her soft features had come alive. Fire blazed in her brown eyes, heat burned brightly in her cheeks and passion had pouted her rosy lips to an enchanting curve.

It would be nice to taste her again, he thought. But he was a busy man and didn't have time for such pleasantries. Besides, he'd not flirted in years. Not since he was a teenager. A few kisses now would lead his body straight toward the main course. Now that he thought about it, he was already straying in that direction. Why had he kissed her like that? He usually waited until he'd dated the woman! And yet, there was something about this particular woman....

"All right. Then maybe you're in the mood for talking," he said as he took a seat a few inches away from her.

She scooted to her left to put an even safer distance between them. "I—I don't think it would do any good to talk now, Mr. Bedford. We'd both be wasting our time."

He studied her for a moment as though he was weighing whether this meeting between them actually held any importance. "Perhaps you're right. But I would like to know one thing. What did you mean when you said you couldn't get me out of your mind? You don't know me."

Before he could see the bewilderment in her eyes, her gaze dropped to a spot on the hardwood floor. "I suppose I didn't phrase that quite right. You're not exactly 'in my mind.' I just see you—at odd times."

His expression said he was completely confused and Claudia couldn't blame him. She'd been confused for days now.

"What does this mean, you see me?"

She made a palms-up gesture with her hands. "I see you. For no reason at all. Your face comes to me out of nowhere."

Baffled, his head swung back and forth. "Correct me if I'm wrong, but when you first walked into this office, you told me we'd never met."

"That's true. We haven't."

"Then how...how did you know what I looked like? You had a picture? Where did you get it?"

"I didn't have any idea what Hayden Bedford looked like until I walked into this office! Look, Mr. Bedford, this isn't...some crazy infatuation and I'm not stalking you. It's nothing like that. I've been—well, I've been very worried and confused because this problem has been going on with me for two or three weeks now and frankly, I want to know why."

"Are you—" He rubbed the heels of his palms against his thighs, then rose to his feet and glanced down at her. "Are you suggesting that you've been seeing me in some sort of—vision?"

She passed a shaky hand over her forehead. "That's exactly what I'm trying to tell you."

He chuckled. Shook his head. Then chuckled again. "Really, Ms. Westfield. This is San Antonio, not the Twilight Zone."

"You don't have to tell me where I am, Mr. Bedford," she said primly.

His blue eyes were full of suspicion as they raked her from head to toe. "How could a vision lead you here? How did you know my name? Am I supposed to believe that I talk to you, too?"

She sighed. This is exactly what she'd been dreading, she thought. Questions for which she had no answers. "No. So far you haven't said anything to me. But I picked up on things in the background. Like your boat. And then it finally dawned on me to trace the numbers through registrations. I can tell you that I was pretty shocked when I found out there was such a boat and an actual person owned it.''

"I keep that boat docked down on the coast at Port O'Connor. You were obviously there and copied the numbers," he accused.

Sadly, she shook her head. "I wish that were true. That would prove I might not be going crazy. But now, after seeing you—seeing that you're the man—I really don't know what to think."

He muttered a curse. "This is ludicrous and if I had any sense at all I'd call the cops and have them check up on you!"

Claudia gestured toward the phone. "Go ahead. If they can explain any of this, I'd gladly welcome their help."

Glaring at her now, he stalked over to his desk, picked up the receiver and shook it at her. "I have a friend who's a detective on the force," he warned.

"Good. That will be even better. He might have some ideas of how to solve this mess."

Seeing he couldn't frighten her into confessing, he slammed the receiver back onto the hook. "Do you realize how stupid you sound? How stupid it makes me look just to be listening to this?"

She nodded. "Yes, I realize."

"People don't have visions. Not normal people. And they certainly don't have them about me!"

Unblinking, Claudia stared at him. "A month ago I would have said you were right. Now, unfortunately, I'm forced to disagree."

He strode back to the couch and, with his thumbs riding his belt, stared down at her. "I don't know what you're after Ms.—"

"Claudia," she interrupted. "You've already kissed me, so you might as well call me by my first name."

He didn't want to call her by any name. And as for kissing her, that had been a big mistake. Because in spite of her lunacy, he wanted to do it again.

"Like I started to say, *Claudia,* I don't know what you're after," he bit out, "but you'll not get anything from me and I mean *anything.*"

Rising to her feet, she met his gaze and as she did so a terrible sadness welled up in her. Yet she could understand his doubts and suspicions. She couldn't blame him for accusing her of being dishonest. She still couldn't quite believe any of this herself. It would be stupid to expect him to swallow such a story.

"Don't worry, Mr. Bedford. This is the last time you'll ever see me."

Politely, she reached to shake his hand and felt a sense of gratitude that he didn't object. "I apologize for taking up your time. Goodbye."

Bewildered by this sudden turn of events, he watched her start toward the door. "What will you do now?" he asked.

Glancing back at him, she shrugged. "Go home and hope that I never see your face again." And she wouldn't, she told herself grimly. If she took off the opal. Claudia had not told this man about the ring. She'd understood it would've only made the whole thing even more far-fetched. And now it didn't matter. She was ending her search. And the visions.

Hayden thought he would feel relief once the woman was out of his office. But now that she was gone, the room felt eerily empty, as though she'd taken the very life out of it.

Raking a hand through his hair, he sank into the comfortable chair behind his desk and reached for the telephone. Halfway there, his hand paused in midair and, with a muffled groan, he flopped back against the seat.

He'd kissed the woman! And not just a peck on the cheek. He'd really kissed her! What had he been thinking? Oh, he'd met women before that he'd been attracted to on first sight, but he'd never impulsively kissed one. In fact, he couldn't think of one woman he'd kissed since he and Saundra had divorced.

That notion was shocking in itself and he quickly leaned up and pushed the button on the intercom connecting him to Lottie's desk.

"Yes, Mr. Bedford."

The fact that the woman called him Mr. Bedford was laughable. She'd been with the company for thirty-five years and during that time she'd seen Hayden born and his father die. She knew everything about the family, including births, deaths, marriages, divorces, public scandals and hidden affairs. But apart from her knowledge of the Bedford family tree, she kept the office running smoothly. No matter if they were experiencing times of joy or strife.

"How long have I been divorced?"

"Three years, sir."

"That long?"

"Yes. Why?"

"I just realized something about myself, that's all."

"Are you ready to start taking your calls now?"

"No. Not yet." He paused and rubbed his chin thoughtfully. "Lottie—"

"Ms. Westfield is staying on the river walk. I have her hotel and room number."

"What makes you think I was going to ask you about her?"

There was a pause and then his secretary said, "I just had a feeling."

"That's a scary thought. The last time you had a 'feeling' crude oil bottomed out to a record low."

"Well, I hardly think Ms. Westfield could have any effect on crude prices."

No, but she'd already had an affect on him, Hayden thought. And he wasn't a bit sure what to do about it.

"Cancel the rest of my calls, Lottie. I'm going out to the site to see Vince and then I'm quitting for the rest of the day."

"What about Ms. Westfield?"

He snatched up a pen. "All right, damn it, give me the hotel and room number. I've got some unfinished business with her."

"What sort of business is she in?"

"Illusions, Lottie."

"Illusions? Did you have a few beers with your lunch, Mr. Bedford?"

"I'm stone-cold sober," he answered. "Although right now the idea of getting drunk has a mighty big appeal."

Inside her hotel room, Claudia snatched up the telephone directory. She was going to call the airport and get the next available flight back to Fort Worth. There was no point in staying in this town any longer. Hayden Bedford was a jerk and she'd been stupid for ever allowing Liz to dare her into making this ridiculous journey.

As for the opal, she'd get rid of it as soon as she got back home. The only thing the ring had ever brought her was a pile of misery. Never again would she allow it to lead her anywhere. Especially to a worthless man!

Claudia was on hold, waiting for the ticket clerk to make a search through scheduling when a knock sounded at the door.

With an impatient groan, she dropped the receiver onto the bed and walked across the room. At the door, she called cautiously, "Who is it?"

"Me. Hayden Bedford."

Claudia was so stunned she grabbed the doorknob and gripped it to keep from falling over.

"What do you want?" she asked warily.

"Not to have this conversation through the door," he said.

Her hands shaking, she unbolted the lock, then opened the panel of wood wide enough for her to see him squarely. "Our conversation was concluded back in your office, Mr. Bedford."

"Call me Hayden. Since you've already kissed me, you might as well use my first name," he said, using her earlier phrase.

"I'm sorry, but I'm on the telephone. I don't have time to talk to you now." *Nor do I have the courage,* Claudia thought. This man made her feel weak, strange and vulnerable. Just looking at him reminded her she was a woman. One who didn't know anything about men like him or how it felt to be in the grip of a passionate love affair.

"I'll wait," he said, then pushed through the open door before she could stop him.

Seeing she didn't have much choice in the matter, Claudia hurried over and snatched up the telephone. Long before she placed the receiver against her ear, she could hear the loud buzz of the dial tone. Damn it, she'd lost her connection!

Dropping the receiver back on the hook, she turned to find he'd helped himself to a seat in a stuffed armchair. As though he had every right to make himself comfortable in her room. She'd never seen anything like him!

You need to correct yourself on that, Claudia. You've seen him before. Too many times.

But those visions hadn't given her a clue to what sort of man she was dealing with, she thought. A picture might speak a thousand words, but the real thing spoke volumes and she was getting the message that Hayden Bedford was a man who usually got his way, even if he had to get it by force.

"What happened? Decided you didn't want to talk now that you had me for an audience?" he asked.

Claudia rolled her eyes. "The call had been disconnected. I'm sure the woman probably hung up when she came back on the line and found I wasn't waiting. Now I'll have to go through the ordeal of making another call."

"Sorry," he apologized. "Was it important?"

"Flight tickets back to Fort Worth!"

"Didn't you buy a round fare to begin with?"

Like a replay in his office, her breathing was growing short again, along with her temper. Which didn't make sense. She tried to be a kind, patient person with everyone, no matter what sex or age. And he really wasn't being that awful.

"Yes. But I want to leave this evening. Now!"

He studied the aggravation on her face and the taut line of her slender body. She'd changed out of the white dress and into a pair of loose navy pants and short red top that exposed her arms and much of her back. The clip was gone from her hair and the honey-brown strands swished against the tops of her shoulders with each little movement of her head. This Claudia Westfield looked far different from the prim woman who'd visited his office. And far more appealing.

"Why the rush?"

Claudia wasn't exactly sure why she felt such a desperate need to run back to Fort Worth. There wasn't anything urgent waiting for her there. Yet the thought of home was consoling. Mainly because she knew there would be no outside chance of having to deal with this man again. Especially after she got rid of the ring.

Claudia twisted the opal around her finger. Once she'd decided to try to solve the mystery of her visions, she'd returned the ring to her hand. But at this moment she was definitely getting the urge to slip it off and keep it off. "My business here is over."

"Meaning me?"

"I guess you could put it that way." She forced herself to look at him. "So why did you come here to the hotel?"

"That's a good question, Claudia. Maybe you can answer that. You say you can see things about me."

The husky tone of his voice cloaked her name in velvet and conjured up images in Claudia's thoughts that were distinctly wicked.

"I'm not a mind reader, Hayden. Not even yours. And I've never had visions before until…well, until a few weeks ago." Disturbed by her outrageous thoughts and his probing gaze, she began to move around the room. "Furthermore, I'm not one of those people that dabbles in the psychic. Physics in the science lab, but never the supernatural."

"I find that hard to believe for a woman who claims to have visions."

She paused long enough to cast him a disgusted glance. "I imagine I find it even more preposterous," she admitted. "I even had a medical checkup in hopes of finding an explanation. The doctor gave me none."

There wasn't the slightest chance in hell that this woman had experienced visions, Hayden thought. He didn't believe in such things. He'd come here because he wanted to know why or how she'd pulled him into this crock. And to see her again, to prove to himself that there was nothing special about her.

"Magic, extrasensory perception, mystical powers— I'm not interested in those things. I'm a down-to-earth man, Claudia. I believe in facts. So the answer I really want from you is, why me? Of the millions of people in the world, why choose me for whatever it is you're doing?"

She walked over to where he sat and made a palms-up gesture as a display of innocence. "I'm not doing anything, Hayden. I'm not here to con you in any way."

He looked unconvinced. "I'm a rich man," he informed her.

The faint frown on her face turned to a glare. "I'm not interested in what your bank accounts look like. But if you're worried that mine are flat, I can give you the names of some financial institutions in Fort Worth that will prove otherwise."

Maybe he should take her up on that, Hayden thought. Yet for some reason he believed that part of her story. The woman hadn't been brought up in poverty. She just didn't have that sort of bearing about her.

"Okay. You're not after my money or my—shall we

call it affections—so what's the deal? And be honest this time.''

Claudia studied the rough, craggy lines of his face and wondered how just the mere touch of his lips against hers had been enough to knock her feet out from under her. Men had never affected her that way. Even Tony, with his smooth looks and practiced lovemaking, had never made her swoon.

Tony had called her frigid. She'd considered herself systematic. All that talk about passion and fire between the opposite sex had seemed like overexaggeration to her. Now, after meeting Hayden Bedford, she wasn't quite so sure.

"Sorry, but I have been honest with you. I came here for your help. Nothing more.''

He raised up to the edge of the chair and stared at her through narrowed eyes. "Help?''

Breathing deeply, she turned her back on him and stared down at the opal on her hand. She desperately wanted to rip it off and order this man out of her room. But something stronger, some intangible force, was preventing her.

"Yes,'' she answered quietly. "To help me figure out exactly why you've barged into my life. If I can find out why, then maybe I can get rid of you. For good!''

"You're making me feel so wanted,'' he said dryly.

"You don't want to feel wanted,'' she muttered. "Not by me.''

Suddenly one of his hands was on her bare back and electric frissons rippled over her skin. Her first instinct was to move away from his touch, but she was frozen, mesmerized by him and the strange things he was doing to her.

"I think the best thing we could do is forget about

this vision thing and get to know one another a little better. Why don't we go down to one of the cafés on the river walk and have dinner? Maybe between the two of us, we can come up with a practical solution.''

Oh, she had a solution, Claudia thought. Simply throw Betty Fay's ring out the window and forget she'd ever possessed such a piece of jewelry. But would that help explain things? Could she go home then and be satisfied that Hayden Bedford had no connection to her life?

"I'm sure you're a busy man. Having dinner with me is unnecessary.''

His hand moved slightly but oh so seductively against her back.

"I'm not so busy that I don't take time to eat.''

The tips of his fingers were toying with her hair and she wondered if he was this intimate with all the women he met over the course of the day. Surely he wasn't. Surely he couldn't find a reason to kiss one of them. Not the way he'd kissed her.

"All right. When is a good time for you?'' she conceded while hoping she didn't sound as breathless as she felt.

"Right now,'' he purred.

She closed her eyes and prayed for the shaking inside her to stop. "Let me call the airport again. I might be able to get a later flight tonight.''

With his hands on her shoulders, he turned her around to face him. "Forget about leaving San Antonio tonight, Claudia.''

"And why should I do that?''

His hands slid up both shoulders, beneath the hair framing her neck, then cupped her face.

"Because I want you to.''

Like a rose suddenly thrust into the desert heat, she

felt herself wilting. If he hadn't been holding her she would have collapsed at his feet.

"Your idea of help isn't exactly what I needed from you," she said.

He chuckled lowly and the sexy sound fanned her cheeks like a tempting caress. "There you go again, reading my mind. Maybe you do have some sort of sixth sense."

He was making fun of her and she hated him for that. Hated him for making her feel so weak and vulnerable. For not understanding how lonely and terrified she'd felt these past weeks.

"Being a woman gives me enough power to read your mind!"

That seemed to sober him and he stepped back as though he couldn't quite believe he'd been holding her in such an intimate way.

"Sorry. Something comes over me when I get close to you," he said, and Claudia could see that the admission shocked him as much as it did her.

"Then we'd better make sure we don't get close," she countered.

With a grim nod of agreement, Hayden motioned her toward the door.

Chapter Three

Once they were out of the hotel room, Claudia began to breathe normally and by the time they were seated at a small, sidewalk café overlooking the river walk, she'd almost convinced herself that she hadn't just taken a leap off the high dive.

"Have you visited San Antonio before?" he asked as the waitress served them their drinks.

Tourists and locals were everywhere in the boutiques and restaurants lining the river. Since it was the height of the dinner hour, Claudia was surprised they'd managed to find a vacant table fairly close to the hotel. It was positioned on a small terrace made of wooden planks. A nearby sago palm dappled the late-evening sun with cooling shadows and secluded them from the main group of diners. Any other time, she would have appreciated the extra privacy, but with Hayden as her dinner partner she would have welcomed the diversion of a noisy family sitting next to them.

"Yes. But it's been a while." She stirred sugar into her iced tea. "Do you live here in the city?"

"A few miles west and south, in the hill country."

"So you commute here to the city to your offices."

He nodded. "Bedford Roustabout has always been headquartered here in the same old building. My grandfather developed the business in the late nineteen forties. When he died my father took over the reins. After I graduated college at Texas University in Austin, I joined him."

"Is your father still helping to run the company?"

He reached for his glass. "No. Unfortunately he died about five years ago."

Claudia had always been close to her parents. They'd provided her with a solid foundation through her childhood and because they'd always been there for her, the idea of losing either one of them had seemed impossible. Until her grandmother Betty Fay had passed away. Her death had jolted Claudia and reminded her that her family was mortal and not something to take for granted.

"That must have been devastating," she murmured.

"It was. He was only in his fifties. He was driving home one night when a drunk ignored a yield sign and smashed into the driver's side of Dad's truck. To make matters worse, I'd lost my mother only a year before that happened."

"In another accident?" she asked, stunned that any one person could be handed such a double dose of grief.

"No. She had a blood disease that had weakened her immune system. She contracted pneumonia and wasn't able to recover." He looked at her over the rim of his tea glass. "What about you? Do you have parents?"

"Yes. In Fort Worth. Not far from where I live."

He smiled as though her answer was what he'd expected. "So you're still close to the nest."

Claudia put down her spoon and leaned back in the wooden chair. He made it sound as though she was still wet behind the ears and needed protecting. "I don't see that you've exactly strayed far from the home range yourself."

He studied her with something like appreciation. "I guess I asked for that, didn't I?"

She shrugged as her expression turned rueful. "Actually, I shouldn't have said that to you. It wasn't exactly nice. Not with your parents being gone."

He chuckled lowly and she was reminded of a few minutes ago in the hotel room. He'd been so close she'd been able to see the green flecks in his blue eyes and the faint shadow of beard threatening to break through his skin. His male scent had enveloped her like a forbidden aphrodisiac and the urge to kiss him a second time had nearly overwhelmed her.

"I don't expect niceness out of people, Claudia. Just honesty. Besides, you didn't say anything to me that I didn't say to you."

Because he was too potent a man to look at for more than a few moments at a time, she turned her gaze to the narrow river. A few feet from their table, a small boat was passing by. A young couple were aboard, hugged close together on the simple seat near the bow. Their foreheads nearly touched as they exchanged words meant only for each other. Clearly, the outside world had been forgotten by the lovers and the sight of them filled Claudia with a strange sort of melancholy.

Most people considered her a cool person, a woman more interested in science and learning than femininity or romance. But at one time she'd believed in love and all the ecstasy that went with it. She'd hoped and believed that somewhere in the world there was a man that was meant to find her and sweep her away, a man who would give her children and love her for the rest of their lives. It was something she longed for and she'd thought, with the help of Betty Fay's ring, she would find him. But Tony had shattered that idea and now it looked as though she was allowing the ring to drag her into another hopeless situation.

"I guess it's a little late to wonder if you're married."

She said the words more to herself than to him, but he answered her just the same.

"If you're feeling guilty about that little kiss we shared, Claudia, then don't. I was divorced three years ago."

Surprised, Claudia looked at him. "You were married?"

"For a couple of years." The corners of his lips turned down with bitter humor. "I guess I was difficult to live with. At least, Saundra thought so." He shrugged. "I left too many dirty socks and wet towels on the floor to suit her."

It was obvious to Claudia that he was making light of the experience to cover up some deeper problem that had gone on between him and his ex-wife. "She didn't divorce you for that reason."

"No. But put a bunch of little things together and you get a big thing. And then there was the fact that Saundra liked men. Young and old. She couldn't waste her life on just one."

"Oh."

"Yeah. Some men have to compete with money. I had to compete with other men. I didn't like that."

Claudia wasn't surprised by his admission. That kiss

he'd given her had tasted more than a little possessive. She'd already decided that once he branded a woman as his, he would expect her to never stray from his range.

"I know all about infidelity, Hayden. It's a humiliating experience. One that I don't ever plan to go through again."

The tart sting of her voice had him searching her face. "What do you know about cheating spouses? You haven't been married, have you?"

She shook her head as the memory of that fateful day she'd walked into Tony's apartment filled her mind. She'd wanted to surprise him with lunch, instead she'd been shocked to find him in the shower with another woman. "You don't have to be married to be cheated on," she said flatly.

He started to say something else, but the sudden appearance of the waitress interrupted him. By the time the young woman served them their meals, he seemed to have forgotten where their conversation had left off and Claudia wasn't about to remind him. The less she remembered that painful episode in her life, the better she liked it.

"You know," he said as he forked up a bite of rib eye steak, "the more I think about this vision thing of yours the more I think there has to be a logical explanation. Are you sure you're not just having daydreams? Sometimes when a person's mind gets tired it wanders off to other things—things that don't necessarily make sense."

The food and the laid-back atmosphere of the open café were beginning to make her feel human again. In fact, if Hayden Bedford hadn't been the image in her visions, she would have been enjoying this time with him. He was unlike any man she'd ever been around and she sensed that, if he was so minded to, he could charm a woman right out of her shoes.

"I'm not dreaming, Hayden. This happens when I'm totally awake and focused."

The fact that she seemed so resolute appeared to irk him. "All right," he conceded, "even if you do 'see' this man, you can't be certain it's me. Could be some old acquaintance or relative in your subconscious thoughts and you just think it's me."

She swallowed a piece of grilled chicken breast, then said, "I've already considered that avenue. I can't think of anyone I know that resembles the man in my visions—except you. Besides, that still wouldn't account for the boat." She frowned as another thought struck her. "Have you ever worn khakis?"

Hayden shook his head. "No. Why?"

"Because I think that's what you're wearing when I see you. But I'm not entirely sure about that. The edges are usually blurred. It's your face that I can see clearly. Or sometimes the boat and the water."

She spoke of the visions in such a cool and collected way that it made Hayden feel uncomfortable. He didn't want to think this woman was flat-out lying to him. Yet there was no way in Hades that he believed in such supernatural nonsense.

"You've been sailing before. Down on the gulf. You've seen the *Stardust* and it stuck in your mind," he reasoned. "Even though she does belong to me, I have to admit she's pretty and would catch most anyone's eye."

"Yes, I agree. The boat has a wooden hull and waxed deck and a carved dolphin at the head of her bow."

"Like I said, anyone would remember her," he countered with a grimace. "Or you could have taken a picture."

"That's true."

She didn't say more and with each silent minute that passed, he grew more and more irritated. "Well? Aren't you going to argue? To deny my theories?"

Claudia studied him calmly. "I'm tired of doing that, Hayden. Your mind is closed and I'd just be wasting my time."

"Look, I thought we came down here to discuss this—to try to find some solution or reason!"

She slipped another bite of food into her mouth. "I thought we did, too. But it's obvious to me that we're headed nowhere."

He put down his fork and reared back in his chair. "Only because you want me to swallow everything you say hook, line, and sinker. Sorry, honey, I'm not that gullible."

Her nostrils flared as she met his dark blue eyes. "And I don't like to be called a liar." She looked away from him, sucked in a sharp breath, then looked back at him. So much for being relaxed, she thought wryly.

"You know, a few minutes with you has made me understand why people are afraid to admit they've seen a UFO. It's not pleasant having someone make you out as an idiot."

"So now you believe in UFOs along with having visions. Lady, you need to put some lead in your shoes and get yourself back down to earth."

It wouldn't do to get angry with him again, Claudia silently told herself. Losing her temper wasn't gaining her anything except a dull headache.

"Sorry to disappoint you, but I haven't mastered the art of floating yet," she said with sarcasm.

What in hell was he doing? Hayden wondered. He was a busy man. There were never enough hours in the day to cover his busy schedule. Yet he'd canceled several pressing phone calls and another appointment just to see this woman again. If he told anyone about this, they'd drive him straight to the mental ward.

Leaning forward, he picked up his fork. "Okay. When you said you wanted my help, just what sort of help were you talking about?"

Her gaze fell from his to the food on her plate. "I'm not exactly sure. I was hoping when I saw you that—" She stopped and shook her head. "Maybe a simple explanation would just fall into place. Dear God, I never expected you to be him!"

"Who did you think I'd be?"

One of her slender shoulders lifted and fell. "Someone connected to the man in my visions. Someone who could lead me to him."

He forked up the last bite of his steak. "Well, you found me. Has it done you any good?"

If anything, Claudia was more disheartened than ever. This narrow-minded man didn't care about her problem or feel any kind of urge to help her. He didn't even believe her!

"Actually, I suppose it has," she said with false cheeriness. "I do know that you're a real person now. And I'm also convinced that you're not supposed to be in my life in any way."

She spoke the last with such certainty that Hayden couldn't help but feel insulted. "Sorry I'm such a disappointment to you."

Suddenly, Claudia couldn't take any more. The past three weeks had drained her and this man's sarcastic indifference was too painful to take. There was no reason to keep putting herself through this.

"I'm sorry, too," she muttered as she jerked the opal from her finger. "Sorry that I ever put this damn ring back on."

She slapped the ring down next to her plate and quickly rose to her feet. "Thank you for dinner, Hayden. I hope you have a happy life."

Hayden wasn't expecting her to just walk away without another word. When she did, he stared after her in stunned silence, then down at the ring she'd left on the table.

"What in hell?"

"Looks like your fiancée doesn't want to be engaged anymore."

Hayden's head jerked around to see that the waitress was standing just behind his shoulders. "Fiancée?" he repeated blankly before it dawned on him that the woman had seen Claudia leave her ring behind. "Uh, actually, I don't know what's wrong with her."

The young waitress looked at him with as much disappointment as Claudia had.

"Then maybe you should go after her?" she suggested.

"Bring my ticket," he told her.

She scurried away without bothering to ask if he wanted a refill of iced tea.

Hayden reached for the ring and studied it with thoughtful scrutiny. The simple piece of jewelry had been worn for a long time. The edges were all smooth; the band in the back worn thin. It didn't make sense that she would leave it, he thought. But then nothing about the woman or his connection to her made any sense.

Dropping the ring into his shirt pocket, he rose to his

feet and tossed enough bills on the table to more than cover the cost of the meal, then headed off in the same direction Claudia had taken before she slipped out of his sight.

Slowing her steps, Claudia glanced around to see that she'd walked much farther than she'd realized. Most of the crowded shops and eating places were behind her. On this particular stretch of the river, only a handful of people were milling about. The quietness was a welcome balm to her shattered nerves.

When she'd left Hayden back at their dining table, she hadn't known where she was going. She'd struck out, walking blindly, not really caring where she went as long as she could be free. Of the ring and the man it had led her to.

So why didn't she feel free? she wondered. The ring was off her hand and gone for good. So was the man. Yet she felt no relief. Instead she was overwhelmed with a sense of loss.

Oh, Claudia, get a grip on yourself. Go home. Forget about Hayden Bedford and the ring. Forget about Gran and her promise of true love. It's not going to happen! Not like this!

Spotting an empty park bench beneath a cypress tree, Claudia sank onto the seat and wiped at the sweat dampening her face and neck. She'd rest for a few minutes, she told herself, then go back to the hotel and call the airport. This time she wasn't going to let anything stop her from getting on the earliest flight she could find. Even if she had to charter one!

"Claudia!"

The sound of her name caused her to jerk. The only person in this city that knew her name was Hayden Bedford. With a sinking feeling, she looked over her shoulder to see him bearing down on her.

"Can't you take a hint?" she asked when he got within hearing distance. "I don't want to see you anymore."

"What about this?" He pulled the ring from his shirt pocket and held it out to her.

Rather than reach to take it, she curled her fingers into a tight fist. "No! I don't want the ring, either. Throw it in the river! It would probably do more good there."

He glanced at the murky water behind him, then thoughtfully dropped the ring back into his pocket.

"You might not want to see me anymore," he said, sinking next to her on the wooden bench, "but I think you owe me an explanation."

She wanted to laugh, but she stifled it. If she let loose one giggle she was afraid she wouldn't be able to stop until she was crying.

"I don't owe you anything. And I think we've both decided there are no explanations for any of this. Not reasonable ones, at least."

His close presence vibrated through every inch of Claudia's body and she was suddenly torn between wanting to cling to the man and wanting to jump and run as fast as she could.

"Forget about those damn visions!" he hissed. "I'm talking about the ring. Are you engaged to someone back in Fort Worth?"

She looked at his face and everything hit her at once. The pain and heartache of Tony's deception. The fear of losing her sanity, and her desperate search for some sort of reason or conclusion to her visions.

"'Engaged'?" she repeated, then began to giggle. "You've got to be kidding! How could I get married?

I'd probably have a vision at the ceremony and try to put the ring on your finger instead of my husband's!'' That idea seemed even more hilarious than her being engaged and though she tried to stifle her giggles behind her hand they kept exploding from her anyway.

Hayden grabbed her by the shoulders. "Stop it!" he ordered. "This isn't funny."

His mutinous face was the final trigger that sent her into shrieks of uncontrollable laughter. "No? I think—oh—oh, Hayden."

Suddenly there were tears on her face and a desperate glaze in her eyes. Hayden didn't understand what was causing her so much agony, but he could see that, at least to her, it was very real. Quickly he pulled her into his arms and pressed her head against his shoulder.

"It's all right, Claudia," he said gently. "Don't cry."

"I can't stand it anymore—I have to get rid of the ring," she said between sobs.

Her warm, slender body was trembling violently against his. He rubbed a hand against her back while smoothing the other over the crown of her hair.

"Don't think about it now," he softly urged. "Put it out of your mind."

The hypnotic movement of his hands and the warm, hard strength of his body slowly worked to calm her. After a few minutes her tears dried to an occasional sniffle and she was able to gather her self-control. But even then Claudia was reluctant to pull back from him. Sheltered in the circle of his arms, she felt totally safe and protected.

"I'm so sorry," she finally murmured. "Histrionics is not the best way to convince you that I'm actually a levelheaded woman."

"Everyone is entitled to a little breakdown once in a

while," he replied. "Besides, I haven't exactly been calm about all of this myself."

The hand against her back was warm and provocative. Claudia could easily imagine it gliding over the rest of her body, searching out every secret curve and nook. She would welcome his fingers upon her skin. Like parched ground beneath a rain, she would soak up his touch and remember it always.

Unsettled by such intimate thoughts, Claudia forced herself to ease away from his embrace. As she fumbled in her handbag for a tissue, she said, "I'd like to get back to the hotel so I can get my bags and head to the airport."

"You don't even have a ticket."

She shook her head. "I'll find some sort of flight heading to Dallas or Fort Worth tonight."

He reached for her hand and squeezed it. "You're not in any shape to be traveling tonight. I want you to come home with me."

Everything inside Claudia went totally still and for a moment she wondered if she was ever going to breathe again. "No—I—"

Her protests were interrupted as Hayden rose to his feet and pulled her along after him. "Don't worry, Claudia. I'm a gentleman. Most of the time."

Color stung her cheekbones. "I wasn't worried about that. I was just wondering—why?"

"Because you still haven't explained all of this to me. And frankly, it would be more comfortable to discuss it there than here in a public place. Besides, staying with me will save you the cost of your hotel room."

It might save her money, but it could shatter her peace of mind, she thought. Or what there was left of it.

"You don't really want to get involved in this and you know it."

He cast her a crooked grin. "From what you've been telling me, you didn't ask to get involved in it, either. But somehow we are."

We. He was finally admitting that he played some part in this strange occurrence and that the two of them were somehow connected. She didn't know whether to feel relieved or wary by his sudden change of attitude.

"Does this mean you've decided to help me? Really help me?"

His expression turned rueful as he reached out and stroked his palm against the side of her face. "I told you before, Claudia, I don't believe in the supernatural. I don't think we're going to find that you've been hexed. But I will do my best to help you get a practical answer to all of this."

He was probably going to show her a little kindness, gain her trust, then try to convince her that the only problem she had was in her head. Well, let him, Claudia thought. She'd welcome the chance to open his eyes, the way hers had been opened the first day she'd had his vision thrust upon her.

"All right. We'll go to your place." She cast him a pointed glance and added, "But just for one night."

With an enigmatic grin twisting his lips, he cupped his hand around her elbow and urged her in the direction of the hotel. "One night is probably all we'll need, Claudia."

Chapter Four

Hayden's home was situated on five acres of rolling hill country far from the lights of San Antonio. Although it was dark when he pulled to a stop in front of the rambling, ranch-style structure, she could see huge oaks shaded the yard and tropical plants grew in tangled splendor next to the stuccoed walls of the house.

As they walked to the door, two large dogs with short yellow hair and faint black markings around their mouths and ears bounded out to greet them.

"What sort of dogs are these?" she asked as they vied for Hayden's attention, then took a few tentative sniffs at her. "They're not Labradors, are they?"

"No. They're black-mouthed curs. They're used for herding cattle."

Deciding the animals wanted to be friends, Claudia took a moment to kneel and pet them. "Oh, do you run cattle?"

"No. The roustabout business keeps me too busy to do any ranching. A friend gave me the dogs as a gift.

But I do loan them out to a nearby rancher from time to time just to let the dogs have fun.''

She raised back up to a standing position. "I'm sure the friend was a woman, right?''

"Friend?''

"That gave you the dogs,'' she explained.

He chuckled as he took her by the arm and led her into the house. "My, my, Claudia, you do see me in the wrong sort of light. I barely have time to eat three meals a day, much less squire a woman. Besides, I've already told you that I only get along with women for brief interludes.''

Claudia looked away from him and hoped he couldn't see her blush in the dim lighting of the foyer. She didn't know what was the matter with her or why she was saying such things to this man. Up until now she'd always respected other people's private lives. She didn't dig into or make assumptions about their personal relationships. But something about Hayden had loosened her tongue.

"Have you always worked such long hours?''

"Not always. I just don't have any reason to cut back my time at work.''

Now that the woman named Saundra had divorced him, Claudia thought grimly. It was odd that she could dislike a person without ever having met her. But then she'd been doing all sorts of odd things this evening, since she'd met this man.

"Come along,'' he said, breaking into her thoughts, "and I'll show you to your room. You might want to freshen up while I fix us something to drink.''

From the foyer, they walked through a long living room with low-beamed ceilings, a Spanish-tile floor and leather furniture. At one end, a long hallway led to a wing of bedrooms. He took her to the furthermost door and flipped on an overhead light.

She stepped into the room while just behind her Hayden placed her bags on the floor.

"It has its own private bath through the door to your left," he said. "Do you think you'll be comfortable here?"

The posted cherrywood bed and matching highboy were something right out of an antique shop. The bed was covered with a patchwork quilt of mostly rose colors and was overlaid with a white bedspread of crocheted lace. Enchanted, Claudia picked up one corner of the bedspread for a closer look.

"The room is beautiful," she assured him, then asked, "is this bedspread handmade?"

"Yes. My mother was talented with her hands. And since her health didn't allow her to do a lot of strenuous outdoor activities, sewing and crafts were something that suited her."

The pride and fond affection that was in his voice told her he was not an indifferent man. Especially where his mother had been concerned. Claudia liked that about him. And the gentle way he'd comforted her back on the river walk.

"It must be nice to have such a beautiful thing to remember her by," Claudia said.

"Yes. She left many things like that behind, but it's her laughter that I most cherish. She was a happy woman in spite of her delicate health." He moved past her and over to a set of French doors bracketed by heavy rose-colored drapes. "If you'd like to go outside, this opens up to a small courtyard. It hasn't been that long since the gardener sprayed for mosquitoes, so I think they'll leave you alone. And if you really feel like a bit of adventure, you can jump in the pool."

"Thank you. But I didn't bring a suit."

One brow arched at her with wry amusement. "Why would you need one? I won't look."

Because he was a gentleman, or because he didn't consider her worth looking at? Claudia wondered.

"Uh, where is your room?" she asked.

Still grinning, he motioned for her to follow him back out into the hallway.

"Right there," he said, pointing to a door directly across from hers. "Not enough distance for you? Or too much?"

Even though his questions shocked her, she tried not to let it show. She didn't want him to think she was naive or intimidated by the idea of spending the night with a man. Especially with one that defined the word "masculine."

"I thought I'd better ask, just to make sure I don't sleepwalk in the wrong direction," she said.

He chuckled. "I'll take pity on you and not ask you which direction would be wrong. Now what would you like to drink? Soda, juice, something stronger?"

After all she'd been through today the idea of something stronger was very appealing. But she didn't want to get too relaxed around this man. She might do something crazy and toss her proper inhibitions out the door.

"Juice would be nice," she told him. "Where will I find you?"

One corner of his mouth lifted in a grin. "You somehow found me in the big state of Texas. Surely you can find me in this little house."

Claudia watched him walk away while mulling over his comment. If he considered this house little, then his statement about being rich had been a very modest description of his financial status. Maybe that was why initially he'd been so wary of her, why he avoided any sort of lengthy relationship to a woman, she pondered. He didn't want to give one a chance to get her claws into his money or assets. Especially if he'd already had to dole out a bunch of it to his ex-wife.

Telling herself that it didn't matter, Claudia went into the bedroom and closed the door.

Five minutes later she found Hayden in a small, efficient kitchen at the back of the house. Two glasses were sitting on a round tray at the end of the cabinet counter. One tall tumbler appeared to be filled with orange juice and crushed ice. The squatty glass beside it contained something that resembled cola. No doubt it was diluting bourbon or rum.

"Let's go out to the screened-in porch," he invited as he picked up the tray of glasses. "It's usually not too hot at this time of the evening."

"Fine," she agreed, then followed him outside.

Once she was settled in a cushioned wicker chair, he handed her the glass of juice. As she sipped it, she looked beyond the screened enclosure to a shadowy yard partially illuminated with a row of footlights. As in the front, it was also shaded with huge, spreading oaks. All around them, the high-pitched singing of frogs and cicadas was intermittently punctuated by the call of a night bird.

"It's very quiet here," she remarked. "Not even a sound of traffic."

"That's what I like after a busy day at work," he said as he took the chair angled toward hers. "The sounds of nature suits me."

"I've always lived in the city," she admitted. "Not having people noises seems strange to me."

He studied her over the rim of his glass. "You never considered living anywhere else?"

Claudia shrugged. "I suppose I've never really taken the time to think about it. For a long time I was focused on getting my teaching degree and then I went to work. Moving away just never was a part of my plan."

"What about the guy—the playboy—weren't you planning to move away with him?"

She mentally cringed and kicked herself for ever admitting something so personal to this man. "He lived in Dallas. That wouldn't have been a major move."

"Where do you teach? A private school in Fort Worth?"

Claudia smiled wanly. "No. Inner-city high school."

He stared at her. "Damn. Didn't anyone ever tell you there's easier places to work?"

"Oh, yes. Many times. That was a major disagreement between me and my parents. I'm not saying they're high society by any means, but they're acquainted with some influential people in the Fort Worth/Dallas area. They could have pulled strings and gotten me a job at any of the more elite private schools. But I didn't want that. I wanted to be where I was needed the most."

He continued to regard her over the rim of his glass. "You must really like kids."

She looked at him. "Why, yes, I do. You and I were both kids at one time. When you were a teenager didn't you want someone to like you, give you special attention?"

He chuckled. "Sure. Girls. And there was one red-headed teacher that really made my heart patter. But unfortunately, she was married."

Claudia shook her head wryly. "I'll bet your parents had to stay on their toes while they were raising you."

"Just part of the time," he admitted with a grin, then his expression sobered and he reached into the breast pocket of his shirt.

Everything inside Claudia went still as he held up the opal ring. "I told you to throw that thing away," she said stiffly.

"But I don't always do what I'm told," he drawled. "And now that we're in the quiet and getting to know one another, why don't you tell me a little more about this ring."

She grimaced. "Believe me, Hayden. You won't like what I have to say."

"I have a feeling you're right about that. But you need to tell me anyway."

Maybe so, Claudia thought, yet she feared his reaction. He was going to label her as crazy. Even worse, he would never look at her in the same way again. Why that should matter so much to her, she didn't understand. Yet it did.

Silent moments began to tick on as she tried to build enough courage to start her story. Across from her, Hayden slipped the ring onto the first joint of his little finger and watched her sandaled foot slice the air. Finally after he'd decided she wasn't going to speak, he said, "You implied you weren't engaged. So I take it this is not an engagement ring?"

She breathed in deeply before she answered. "No, it was a gift. Given to me four years ago on my twenty-first birthday."

"From a man?"

Laughter slipped past her lips. "No. Not from a man. From my grandmother. Betty Fay Westfield. The ring had belonged to her for many years. We—the family, I mean—don't know where she got it. She never would tell us. But we all pretty much concluded it was given to her by a man.''

''Hmm. Then I'm surprised you'd want to throw it away,'' he mused out loud. ''Or maybe you didn't like your grandmother all that much.''

That woke her up and she leaned forward in her chair to search his face in the muted light. ''I loved Gran. She and I had a special bond. I guess that's why she gave me the ring. She thought she was doing something special for me. Turns out…well, I wished she'd given it to someone else. Like maybe one of her enemies.'' She muttered the last few words.

''Why is that?''

The opal seemed to glow against his darkly tanned skin and for one hysterical moment Claudia wondered what would happen if the ring caused him to have a vision. Or did the damn thing only work on her? she wondered.

''Because it's brought me nothing but trouble.''

''What sort of trouble? A little elaboration here might help get to the root of the problem.''

She glared at him faintly. ''I don't know exactly how to describe the problem. You might simply call it man trouble.''

He groaned, then pensively rubbed his thumb and forefinger against the middle of his forehead. ''So what you're telling me is that this little ring somehow caused you to have a string of bad affairs with men?''

She gasped with indignation. ''I've never had an affair in my life!''

He simply looked at her.

She squared her shoulders and tucked her hair behind

her ears. "Well, I had an emotional relationship with Tony," she conceded. "But that's all. And that would have never happened if it hadn't been for the ring!"

"Ah, the ring." He held up his finger and looked at it with feigned awe. "Somehow this little piece of jewelry made you fall in love with the wrong guy."

"That's exactly right! Now we're getting somewhere."

"Yes. I thought so, too," he drawled softly. "Until now."

Groaning with frustration, she looked up at the slanted rafters above their heads. "Maybe I need to go back to the very beginning. Otherwise there's no hope of you ever understanding."

Hayden figured she could go back to the point where God created Eden and he still wouldn't understand. But he didn't express the negative feeling to her. She was talking. And he figured if he let her rattle on for long enough, she'd finally slip and spill the whole truth about her visit to his office.

"I'd say that's a good idea. Start at the beginning and don't leave anything out," he encouraged.

Leaning back in the chair, Claudia crossed her legs again and tried to appear relaxed instead of as a woman whose nerves were about to snap at any moment.

"Okay. To begin with, every friend and relative of Betty Fay's knew the ring was special to her. Which was odd to begin with when the woman had scads of diamonds and other expensive jewelry."

"Your grandmother was rich?"

"Very. But not always. She and Grandfather made a fortune in the concrete business. The boom of the fifties was a good time to be connected to the construction business."

"Wait a minute," he said, "didn't anyone ever stop to ask your grandfather if he gave her the ring?"

Claudia shook her head. "No one knew about the opal until after he'd died and that was before I was born. He was a chain smoker and suffered a fatal heart attack by the time he reached forty-five."

"So you don't think the ring came from him?"

"No. If so, she would have worn it while he was alive. And another thing, he wouldn't have given her something so—well, inexpensive."

"Big spender?"

"From what my mother said, he spoiled Gran with the very best." Shrugging one shoulder, Claudia continued. "But she considered this opal to be a lot more precious than any of her diamonds. So much so that she believed it had special powers."

Hayden laughed. "Powers? You mean like hocus-pocus magic stuff?"

His laughter was offensive, even though she understood how ridiculous this must sound to him. "Who knows what she actually meant. All I know is that when she gave me the ring, she told me to wear it and I'd find my true love." She grimaced. "Two days after I started wearing the ring I was walking through the mall and it slipped from my finger and started rolling across the hard tile. Before I could catch up to it, the thing rolled right between Tony's feet and stopped as though it had a mind all its own. When he plucked up the opal and placed it back in my hand, I thought it was kismet."

Hayden looked at the ring and then at Claudia. After a moment he smiled with understanding. "I get it now. When you got tangled up with the playboy you thought you'd found Mr. Right. And when it turned out he was Mr. Wrong, you blamed it on the ring."

"Not exactly. I blamed myself for not using more common sense."

He nodded. "That was good, practical thinking."

Her jaw grew rigid, her eyes narrowed. "I thought so, too. That's why I put the ring away and pretty much forgot about men."

How could a woman as young and beautiful as her forget about men? Hayden wondered. It was unnatural. Not to mention unhealthy.

"I wouldn't say you needed to go that far," he said.

One corner of her lips twisted with bitter resignation. "When you've been deceived you lose your self-confidence, you feel stupid for letting yourself be duped. I'm not sure I can ever trust myself to be smart enough to pick the right man for me."

Saundra's cheating ways had left Hayden feeling the same way. Since his divorce, he'd been afraid to trust himself with another woman, much less trust her. Yet hearing Claudia admit to having such an embittered attitude seemed all wrong.

"If you feel that way, why were you wearing the ring when you came to my office?" He wanted to know.

"I put it on to honor my grandmother on what would have been her eighty-first birthday," she answered, then shrugged. "After all, I was pretty sure the ring didn't possess any sort of powers. Not since I'd learned my lesson with Tony." Her eyes were full of agony as she looked over at him. "But I didn't know—I never dreamed anything like this would happen."

"Anything like this?" he prodded.

Claudia's breathing grew shallow as his eyes probed her face.

"The visions," she said in a hoarse whisper. "The ring makes me have visions. Of you."

He wanted to laugh. He needed to laugh so that she could see how inane her statement sounded to him. Yet he couldn't force even one little chuckle past his lips.

"You actually expect me to believe that?"

His quietly spoken question was full of accusation and Claudia realized with a heavy heart that the two of them were going around in a useless circle.

"Not really. But you asked for the truth and the story behind the ring. I warned you that you weren't going to like it."

"I don't," he clipped. Ice tinkled as he tossed back the last of his drink, then set his glass on a low table to the right of his chair. "I don't like having someone insult my intelligence. Especially a woman."

She sighed. "I knew it was a mistake to come here with you," she muttered. "But I thought you'd changed your mind. I thought you'd decided…well, that you actually wanted to help."

The disappointment ringing through her voice only irritated Hayden even more. Saundra had been good at concocting stories and expecting him to be sucker enough to believe them. She'd also been good at acting hurt and offended. It bothered him, more than he cared to admit, that Claudia was trying to pull the same thing with him.

Yet she sounded so truthful, he thought, so troubled, that he wanted to believe her. Damn it all.

"Have you stopped to ask yourself how all this sounds?" he asked. "The Roswell incident back in 1947 is more believable than this stuff you're trying to heap on me."

Agitation pushed Claudia to her feet and she quickly walked to one end of the screened enclosure. Staring out at the night shadows, she said, "I'm sorry I don't have any sort of documented proof to give you. My grandmother is dead and the ring can't talk. So that just leaves me and it's obvious I'm not a very convincing person.''

She heard him leave the chair and her body tensed with anticipation as he came to stand behind her left shoulder.

"Look, Claudia, if you have some romantic notion—though God only knows why you would—that this ring led you to me, you'd best go home and forget it. I've already had one marriage partner. I'm not looking for another one. In fact, I don't have plans to have a woman in my future for any reason.''

His arrogant assumption inflamed her and she whirled on him. "Evidently you haven't been listening to a thing I've been telling you! I have no romantic notions anymore! Not about you. Not about any man.''

"You came to San Antonio—''

The remainder of his sentence was interrupted as she poked a finger in the middle of his broad chest.

"Do I look like a woman who's so desperate she has to fly hundreds of miles just to find a man to give her romantic attention?''

"Not exactly, but—''

"For your information there are men in Fort Worth who find me attractive,'' she practically yelled. "Some of them would probably even consider proposing marriage to me. But marrying one of them doesn't interest me any more than marrying you does. I came to San Antonio to find out why that damn ring makes me see you! And that's the only reason.''

She was seething and the fire in her eyes lit her whole face with angry passion. As Hayden's gaze settled on her trembling lips, he realized he'd never wanted to kiss any woman the way he wanted to kiss Claudia at this moment.

"So you say."

The huskily spoken taunt momentarily blinded her with fury and she didn't notice the downward descent of his head until it was too late. Before she could step aside, his hands were gripping her shoulders and his lips were moving hungrily over hers.

Instantly Claudia shouted at herself to pull away from him, to show him that his touch, his words, meant nothing to her. But something overcame her. Something hot and wild and impossible to resist.

Her hands fluttered against his chest, her mouth opened against the rough insistence of his lips. The next thing she knew his tongue was inside, stroking, daring her to give in to him and the pleasure he was giving her.

A helpless moan sounded in her throat and her fingers curled into the front of his shirt. Sensing her surrender, Hayden circled one arm around her waist and the other across her back. By the time her body was crushed up against his, he was totally lost, completely intoxicated by the taste of her lips, the heat of her soft curves.

Mindless to everything but him, Claudia slid her arms upward to circle his neck. The movement thrust the mounds of her breasts into his chest and positioned the juncture of her legs directly against the already aching mound in his jeans.

The intimate contact shocked him with intense pleasure and he gripped her hips with his hands and buried his lips in the side of her throat.

"Claudia," he whispered thickly, "what are you doing to me?"

The desire in his voice stunned Claudia. Almost as much as the raging need she felt to get closer to this man. This wasn't supposed to be happening, she thought wildly. Wanting to make love to this man wasn't a part of her plans!

"Hayden! This is..." Sweet sensations rippled through her as his lips nibbled at her throat. "I didn't come here for this."

"No," he murmured as he kissed his way back to her lips, "but something is telling me that this is exactly what we're intended to do."

The ring! It was causing them to fall into each other's arms this way. She couldn't let it happen. She couldn't let it push her into another heartbreaking mistake.

"No, Hayden!"

With a desperate little moan, she managed to twist herself out of his arms and put a marginal space between them.

Still gripped with desire, Hayden stared at her in confusion. "Claudia—"

When he started toward her, she immediately stepped back. "Give me that ring," she ordered hoarsely.

"What?"

"The ring. Take it off and give it to me so that I can throw it away!"

He looked blank for a moment, then down at the ring that was encircling the first joint of his little finger. "You don't think—oh, Claudia, come on," he said with disbelief. "You don't think this ring had anything to do with us, do you?"

"If you're talking about what just happened between us, then yes, I do! And I'm going to get rid of it before anything else can happen!"

She held out her hand, but he made no move to give her the ring. Instead he pulled it off his finger and tossed it toward the table where he'd left his whiskey glass.

Claudia watched as the ring missed the piece of furniture and clattered across the dark floor.

"You naive little thing! A man doesn't need a charm piece to induce him to make love to a woman! And now that the damn thing is out of the way, I think you need to learn just that!"

Not daring to trust herself or her theories about the ring, she took several more steps back from him. "No. I know what's causing all of this. Even if you don't."

His eyes glinted back at her and for a moment she likened the light to the iridescent glow of Betty Fay's opal.

"If you're so sure, then you shouldn't be afraid to put it to the test," he taunted.

At this moment Claudia wasn't certain of anything. Except that she had to get away from this man and tomorrow morning wouldn't be any too soon.

"I'm not afraid," she said stiffly. "I'm just being practical."

He stepped toward her and, even though she knew if he touched her she would melt like a piece of chocolate candy, she steeled herself to hold her ground.

"Practical," he repeated with sarcasm. "I think we've just discovered the cause of your *man* problem, Claudia. And all this time you've been trying to hide it behind a little ring."

He couldn't have said anything that would have hurt her more. Tony had accused her of being frigid and unromantic. And when she'd refused to go to bed with him, he'd turned to other women. Now Hayden was accusing her of the same thing.

Her lips began to tremble as tears gathered at the backs of her eyes. "Maybe you're right, Hayden," she said in a low, choked voice. ''Maybe I'm not woman enough to…to make love to any man!''

Before he could react, she fled past him and into the house.

Cursing, Hayden went after a flashlight to search for the ring.

Chapter Five

Early the next morning Hayden stood at the cookstove as he gave the eggs one last stir, then ladled them from the skillet onto a warm plate that was already filled with several slices of bacon and toast. After loading the plate on a tray, he completed the meal with a glass of orange juice, a cup of coffee and a tiny pitcher of cream. He didn't go so far as to place a fresh flower on the tray. But he did lay the opal ring atop a folded napkin in one corner.

At her bedroom door, he knocked lightly and called, "Claudia, are you awake?"

Immediately the door opened and Hayden was surprised to see that she'd already gotten out of bed and showered. Her brown hair was wet and slicked straight back from her face. A pale pink chenille robe was wrapped around her slender curves. As she tightened the sash at her waist, her brown eyes wavered suspiciously from his face to the tray in his hands.

"I made you a little breakfast," he said, feeling more awkward than he could ever remember.

"I see," she said coolly.

She made no move to accept the tray or to invite him in and a part of Hayden didn't blame her. He'd behaved like a jackass last night. In fact, he was still wondering what had come over him. He wasn't a man who went around pressuring a woman. Especially since Saundra had just about chilled all his sexual desire. But last night he'd suddenly gotten this feeling that he'd known Claudia all of his life and that he wanted her with every fiber of his being. He'd never felt such an instant, all-consuming urge in his life. If she hadn't stopped the embrace, he would have ended up carrying her straight to his bed. And if he didn't know better, he would almost believe that damn ring of hers had done something strange to him.

"Uh, are you hungry?"

Nodding, she opened the door wider for him to enter the room.

"You didn't have to go to the trouble of bringing the meal to me. I was about to get dressed and come to the kitchen," she told him.

"It's no trouble," he said, but he didn't add that he'd never served anyone this way. He wasn't exactly sure why he was doing it for her, except that he wanted to make up for any hurt he might have caused her last night.

"Where would you like to eat. In bed? Or maybe out on the patio?"

Claudia glanced at the bed with its wrinkled covers. She'd already spent too much of the night fighting images of Hayden Bedford. No way was she going to get back into that bed with him in the room with her.

"The patio would be nice," she said, and quickly crossed the room to open the French doors.

Outside, a paving of red brick led to a low wooden deck shaded by a giant weeping willow. Claudia was instantly enchanted to discover a white wrought-iron table positioned in one corner. Two matching chairs were pushed beneath the glass top.

He placed her food on the table, then pulled out both chairs. After she was seated, he joined her on the opposite side.

"What time do you have to be at work?" she asked as she stirred cream into her coffee. "Do I need to eat quickly?"

He studied the subtle colors and soft, smooth textures of her clean face. If possible, she was even more beautiful this morning, he thought. And he couldn't help but wonder what it would be like to lie with her head pillowed next to his, to see her face flushed with passion.

"There's no hurry," he answered as he tried to fix his thoughts elsewhere. "Lottie will keep things calm until I get there. Besides, I didn't think you'd be leaving this morning."

She lifted her head to stare at him in total disbelief. "You didn't think I'd be staying, did you? I told you yesterday I would stay for one night. And you seemed to think that would give us plenty of time."

"I was wrong."

His admission clearly disconcerted her. She fumbled with her fork before she finally managed to lift a bite of eggs to her lips.

"I was wrong, too," she admitted after a moment. "To ever come here. Or to think you really—"

"Please don't start throwing those accusations at me again, Claudia. I already feel bad enough as it is." Actually, Hayden felt like hell and once he got to the office, he figured Lottie would tell him he looked like it, too. But what did he expect? he wondered ruefully. After spending most of the night rolling restlessly from one side of the mattress to the other, he'd probably done well to get three hours of sleep.

Surprise widened her eyes and formed her lips into a perfect little circle. "You do?"

He grimaced. "Why wouldn't I? I know I behaved like a jerk last night. Ring or no ring, I said some awful things to you. And for what it's worth I don't go around coming on to women the way—well, I never meant for things to get so out of control between us."

Disturbed by his attempt at an apology, her gaze dropped to her plate. The sight of the food made her realize just how much trouble he'd taken to prepare her breakfast. The coffee was smooth, the bacon fried to a perfect golden crisp. The eggs were moist and light, and half of the buttered toast was spread with strawberry jam.

She'd never had a man do anything like this for her before and in a way the gesture seemed almost as intimate as his kiss. The idea sent a blush of heat across her cheeks as she murmured, "I'm sure you didn't mean for it to happen. You just couldn't help yourself."

The frown on his face deepened. "Why? Because you think I'm lecherous?"

Lifting her head, she met his gaze with hard resolution. "No. Because of the ring."

He groaned in protest. "Oh, Claudia, haven't you ever taken a look at yourself in the mirror?"

"Everyday before I go to school. I'm an average, normal-looking woman. Not a Hollywood siren." And she definitely wasn't the sort that made men lose their heads with passion. That rueful thought had her covertly studying his strong face and the powerful body attached to it. This morning he was dressed in a classic Oxford shirt of pale yellow and dark, western-cut slacks. A bola tie fashioned from silver and green malachite and black cowboy boots told her he had his own style and standards. In short, he was the epitome of a tough Texas businessman and there was no doubt in her mind that women turned to look at him as she was looking now.

"For your information, Claudia, there are some men in this world that aren't attracted to sirens. They're drawn to quieter, gentler beauty."

Claudia was trying to decipher that remark when her straying eyes caught sight of the ring at the corner of the breakfast tray. In the shaded morning light it seemed like a harmless piece of jewelry. In fact, it seemed ludicrous that she'd formed such far-fetched notions about the opal. Yet she knew with all her heart that the visions were real and she had only to slip the ring back on to experience another one.

"I thought you threw that thing away," she said, gesturing to the ring.

Hayden's expression turned sheepish. "I thought I had. I searched the back porch for the better part of an hour before I finally found it between a crack in the floorboards."

The idea of him spending so much time looking for the ring totally dismayed Claudia. He didn't believe in its powers. "Why did you bother? I'm going home this morning and we're both going to forget this whole thing."

Hayden watched her bite into a piece of toast as if she was dismissing the matter completely. And if he had any common sense at all, he told himself, he'd get up and dance a jig of relief. But something had happened to him since she'd walked into his office. In some unexplainable way, his life had changed. It was as if she'd come along and brought him out of a deep sleep and now that he was awake again, he was seeing the world in a whole different light. He had to find out why.

"You can't."

A frown marred her face as she chewed the toast. "I'm damn well going to try."

"What happened to the woman who wanted answers? You traveled all the way to south Texas to find me, now you're going to give up after one day?"

"And night," she reminded him ruefully.

Leaning toward her, he folded his forearms across the tabletop. "Is that why you want to leave?" he asked softly. "Because of last night—the way we were together?"

The movement of his body dragged her eyes once again to his broad shoulders and deep chest. She wanted to touch him again, she realized, and kiss him in the same reckless way she had last night. The idea caused her to shiver inwardly.

"We were—under some sort of spell."

"You don't believe in spells and neither do I," he said.

"Then what would you call it? Lust?"

For a split second Hayden was inclined to agree with her. Blaming their little interlude on lust was the easy, sensible way to reason it away. But he couldn't honestly admit, at least to himself, that physical desire was all he'd been feeling for Claudia. There'd been some intangible force drawing him to her and Hayden was half afraid that same force was making him want to keep her here.

Rising to his feet, he jammed his hands into his pockets and looked down at her. "A temporary lapse of sanity. And if you're worried it will happen again, it won't."

Why should she worry? she wondered glumly. He might consider her pretty, but underneath it all he believed she was a cool, practical woman. One not nearly fiery enough for a man like him.

"I'm not worried," she said bluntly. "I just don't see any need to stay longer."

Ignoring her comment he said, "There's a car in the garage and I've left the keys on the kitchen bar if you'd like to drive into the city for any reason. Otherwise, I'll be home this evening."

She looked at him with disbelief. "What am I supposed to do in the meantime?"

"Why don't you try writing down everything you can remember seeing in your visions. And we'll start from there."

Her fingers touched her throat as she stared at him in stunned fascination. "You mean, you've decided to take me seriously?"

No, Hayden thought, he'd decided to take her any way he could get her. Out loud he said, "Yeah. Seriously."

A pleased smile suddenly lit her face. "All right. I'll stay."

The relief he felt was so immense it actually scared him and as he walked away, he wondered if he'd just hung himself.

"I don't like the sound of this, Claudia. Neither will your father. You don't know this man! I can't believe you spent the night with him!"

Her mother's voice was so loud that Claudia was

forced to pull the receiver back from her ear. "Mom, I didn't sleep with the man."

"But what if he'd tried to seduce you?"

Claudia rolled her eyes. She'd waited nearly all day to make this call simply because she'd expected her mother's reaction to be overly dramatic and so far Marsha wasn't disappointing her. "Have you ever thought I might want to be seduced by a man?"

"No. You take great pleasure in periodically reminding me that you're finished with men."

Actually, she'd never really *started* with men, Claudia thought, but at this moment she wasn't in the mood to point that out to her mother. "Mom, I called to let you know where I'm staying so that you won't worry about me."

"But I am worried, honey. First these crazy visions of a man and now you say you've found someone who looks exactly like him. It doesn't make any sense. I'd feel a lot better if you'd just come on home and let me and your father take care of you. We'll get you the best psychiatrist we can find."

Claudia would be the first person to agree that people suffer mental disorders for one reason or another. Just like any other organ, the brain could become sick, too. But now that she'd traced the boat registration and discovered it actually belonged to a real person, she knew she wasn't mentally deranged.

"I don't need a psychiatrist, Mom. Hayden and I are going to get to the bottom of this."

"Claudia, I really—" She broke off quickly, then started again on a different course. "How long do you plan to stay with this man?"

"I'm not sure. I guess it depends on how things progress."

Her mother heaved out a long breath. "Well, I'd feel better if he was married with children."

Not if she knew about that lustful little episode on the porch last night, Claudia thought.

"Don't worry, Mom. I'll keep in touch. And if we do discover anything about the ring, I'll let you know."

"That ring!" she blurted in Claudia's ear again. "You're probably going to find out that Betty Fay bought it from some voodoo shop down in New Orleans. It was probably laying right next to the chicken feet!"

"Goodbye, Mom," Claudia said, then hung up before her mother could belabor the point.

"Lottie, do you believe in destiny?"

The older woman glanced at Hayden's boots that, at the moment, were propped on the corner of her desk. "Yeah, if you don't get some work done around here, we're destined for bankruptcy."

With a weary chuckle, he pulled his folded hands from behind his head and eased his feet back onto the floor. "I had a bad night, Lottie. And I've been on the telephone most of the day. Be kind to me."

The bony, gray-haired woman put down her pencil and took a long pointed survey of his face. "What kind of night did Ms. Westfield have? I hope she looks better than you."

"Lottie! I'm shocked that you would say such a thing!"

The older woman let out a mocking snort. "Nothing about the opposite sex has shocked you since you were five years old."

"Well, if you really want to know, Ms. Westfield spent the night at my house. In her own bedroom," he added grimly.

"What's the matter? Slipping in your older years?"

He glared at his secretary. "She's not that kind of woman."

Lottie picked up her pencil and went back to copying a series of numbers onto a ledger sheet. "All of us women are *that* kind when the right man gets next to us."

Then he must not be the right man for Claudia, Hayden thought. Still, for those few minutes she'd been in his arms, he'd never felt so connected to anyone.

Thoughtful now, he said, "I never knew you liked men, Lottie."

Without bothering to look up, she said, "I love men. I just never found one I wanted to love on a continual basis. Which is a sad thing, Mr. Bedford."

"Why? A person doesn't have to have a spouse to be happy," he told her. "Look at me, for instance. I'm much happier now that Saundra isn't making my life miserable."

She glanced up, her expression saying she was clearly unconvinced. "No, look at me. I'm sixty-five and alone. The closest thing I'll ever have to grandkids will be your children, providing you ever have any."

Lottie's talk of rearing a family turned his thoughts once again to Claudia and he wondered if she'd dismissed all plans of ever being a wife and mother. Maybe she'd decided being a career woman was enough to keep her happy.

"Ms. Westfield had a bad experience with a man," he revealed to his secretary. "She says she doesn't want to get involved with another one."

Lottie's brows inched upward. "Then what's she doing with you?"

Smiling, Hayden rose to his feet, then leaned across

the desk and patted Lottie's cheek. "That's what I've got to figure out."

Claudia was standing in front of the kitchen cabinets, wondering if she should attempt to cook some sort of evening meal, when a sound on the back porch caught her attention. Moments later, the door opened and Hayden stepped in carrying a flat cardboard box.

The moment he spotted her, a wide smile spread across his face. "Well, it is nice to come home to a beautiful woman!"

Claudia tried not to blush or to smile, but in the end she couldn't prevent either. Seeing him again was filling her with a warm pleasure she couldn't deny.

"Hello, Hayden."

"Hello, yourself," he greeted warmly.

"It smells like you brought supper with you," she said as she sniffed the mouthwatering aroma of hot pizza. "Before you walked in I was wondering if I should try to cook something."

"Try?" he asked with humor. "You mean you don't know how to cook?"

She shrugged. "Well, enough to get by. I was always more interested in doing experiments in the kitchen than making a meal."

"Hmm. Sounds like you grew up a regular little scientist, rather than the busy homemaker," he said as he walked over and placed the pizza box on the small bar that extended from one end of the oak cabinets.

"Madam Curie interested me more than Betty Crocker." She went to stand beside him. "I can set the table or get the drinks, if you'd like."

"Set the table," he told her. "And I'll get us some sodas."

Five minutes later they were seated at a small wooden dining table. To their right a row of windows overlooked a portion of the backyard where mockingbirds and gray mourning doves flittered from the lush lawn to a tall bird feeder hidden among a vine of Texas yellow bonnets.

Hayden's home continued to surprise Claudia. All along she'd expected he lived like a traditional bachelor where the essentials were all that mattered. Such as a stove, refrigerator and bed. And a couch for TV watching. Yet this house was the complete opposite. It was a true home in every sense of the word.

"Is this where you lived with your wife?" she asked as they munched through their first slices of pizza.

"No, Saundra and I lived in the city. In a town house. This place was where my parents lived." He cast her a curious glance. "Why do you ask?"

She shrugged while a veil of pink color washed her cheeks. "It seems so homey. Not anything like where a bachelor would live. Even the yard is like an extension of the house."

"Well, I can't take credit for the furnishings or decorations. Mom took care of that. And Dad liked to garden. He also enjoyed the wildlife out here in the country. That's why you see all the bird and squirrel feeders around the yard. He gave up on trying to grow a vegetable garden, though. The deer and the coons always ate everything before it could be harvested," he added with a wan smile.

"You must miss your parents terribly," she said, her heart aching for his loss.

He nodded. "Right after Dad died I started to sell this property—the memories in these rooms were a constant reminder of all that I'd lost. But when it came right down to it, I just didn't have the heart. Then a few years later, right after my divorce, I decided I was glad I hadn't sold. I was sick of living in the city and this place had always suited me."

"What about the memories? They don't hurt now?"

His pensive expression was full of fondness. "No. They comfort me. Because they're all good memories."

"Then you're fortunate."

He looked at her as though her observation surprised him. "You're right. But it took me a while to realize that. For a long time I was pretty bitter about losing both my parents. I kept wondering why other people got to see their mother and dad live to be in their eighties or even nineties. I felt cheated. I felt like I'd been punished for some reason. But later...I realized I was thinking all wrong."

Claudia cast him a gentle, knowing smile. "You were thinking how blessed you really were to have had good parents. Even if it was for a shorter time than most."

He nodded, then picked up a second slice of pizza. "I'm sure a lot of your students come from torn and dysfunctional families."

"Too many," she said grimly. "That's why I chose to teach inner city. Someone needs to care. I realize I'm only one person, but at least I feel good about what I'm doing."

His blue eyes scanned her face as though he were seeing a different woman than the Claudia Westfield he'd first met in his office. "And that's important to you."

She reached for her soda glass. "You say that like it surprises you," she said.

A wry grin touched his lips. "I guess it does. Most of the women I've known are very materialistic. One in particular."

"Your ex-wife?"

His gaze drifted away from her to settle on a pair of doves perched on the top rail of the yard fence. "Yeah. Saundra. Don't get me wrong, she was ambitious. She worked hard at her job. But not because she found it rewarding. She liked what the money could do for her."

"From the looks of Bedford Roustabout, I wouldn't have thought she needed the extra salary," Claudia said.

Hayden frowned. "We didn't need the extra salary. But staying home every day was not Saundra's style. She loved to be out and going and I respected her wishes. She had every right to a career as I did."

"What did she do?"

"She was an office manager for a large insurance company in San Antonio."

"What about children?"

He turned his gaze back to her and Claudia glimpsed a shadow of regret in his blue eyes. "We never got around to having children. She kept promising to get pregnant whenever her job smoothed out. But that never happened. I guess it's a good thing. After I discovered she was being unfaithful, we divorced."

Claudia was suddenly reminded of the crushing pain she'd felt when she'd learned of Tony's infidelity. She'd been thinking of marriage. She'd been thinking she was the love of his life. When actually she'd been little more than a diversion.

"Does your ex-wife still live in San Antonio?"

"No. Someone told me that she's in Austin now."

"Do you miss her?"

His lips twisted into a mocking slant. "You don't miss a migraine, Claudia. You just thank your lucky stars you don't have it anymore."

Yes, she was thankful she'd gotten rid of Tony before

he could cause her any more emotional damage. Once he was out of her life, she'd not missed him. Still, she couldn't let herself forget the pain and the lesson he'd given her.

For the next few minutes they finished the meal in silence. Afterward, Claudia cleaned the small mess from the table while he made a pot of coffee. Once it was finished dripping, they agreed to brave the evening heat and carried their cups outside to a group of redwood lawn chairs situated beneath a giant live oak tree. Nearby, the sleeping cowdogs lifted their heads with interest, but after a moment they must have both decided it was too hot to move from their bed in the shade to do any socializing and their heads flopped back against the thick grass.

"So what did you do to occupy your time today?" he asked after he and Claudia were both seated.

Since they'd eaten, the sun had gone down, but the air was stagnant with humid heat. Above their heads, storm clouds were starting to roll and churn. In a matter of minutes Claudia expected to hear the rumble of thunder. Living in an area where tornadoes were a constant threat had given her a healthy concern for the weather, but the idea of an approaching storm seemed to pale against the turbulent feelings Hayden generated in her. She'd never met any man that could charm her and anger her at the same time, until she'd met this one.

"I did what you suggested and made a list," she said.

For a moment his face was blank and then he looked at her with surprise. "So where is it? I want to know exactly what it is you think you've seen."

Frowning, she eyed him with disapproval. "I don't like the way you phrased that. As though you still don't believe me."

He made a palms-up gesture with his free hand. "I don't believe you. But that doesn't mean I'm not going to take this seriously. So go get the list."

"I don't have to go get it. I can tell you everything I have written on it." She nervously fingered the hem of her cotton tank top. Each time the visions or the ring was mentioned, the two of them ended up in some sort of confrontation. She didn't know if her sanity could survive another one. Especially if she ended up in his arms. "There's not that much."

"Okay, then tell me. What have you seen, besides my face?"

Claudia leaned back in the chair and closed her eyes so that the images around her didn't interfere with her memory. "The boat with its white sails. The dolphin on the bow and the name and number on the side of the hull. And there's lots of water all around."

"The Gulf of Mexico is a lot of water," he conceded.

She opened one eye at him. "Are you being condescending?"

He sipped his coffee. "No. But I've already told you where I keep the *Stardust,* so you know there's a lot of water around it. Besides, it's a foregone conclusion that a boat is going to be near a lot of water."

Claudia looked at him with both eyes. "Look, I'm trying to tell you what was in my visions before I ever came to San Antonio. Do you want to hear about it or not?"

She was being deadly serious when all Hayden really wanted was an excuse to sit here and enjoy her company. He'd spent most of the day looking forward to this evening, knowing that she would be here and the house would seem alive again. He knew that sort of thinking was unwise. Saundra had already taught him that trusting a woman could prove to be mighty painful. And this whole situation with Claudia Westfield should be making him doubly cautious. But there was something about her that charmed him, lured him like the sweet, mysterious scent of a night flower.

"I do. Go on," he said.

Closing her eyes once again, she said, "I think that's everything about the boat that I can remember except that it's wooden and has a small cabin."

Half expecting her to start detailing the cabin, Hayden eased up in his chair and looked at her. But when she spoke again, it wasn't about the boat but something entirely different.

"Sometimes I see a huge white house. It's a two-story and there's a balcony or a widow's walk on the top floor. A porch runs the length of the front and is supported with square pillars. Melon-colored hibiscus are growing nearby. It looks old, but restored in perfect condition. Sort of like one of those old homes that are turned into bed-and-breakfasts. Does this place sound familiar to you?"

Hayden shook his head. "Not at all. I've never stayed in a bed-and-breakfast or a big, white, two-story house. Whenever I travel I stay in hotels or motels."

"What about when you were small and visited relatives?"

Hayden thought for a moment. "No. We visited relatives and friends at times, but I don't recall a house like that."

A sigh of disappointment passed her lips. "Oh, I was hoping the house would give us something to work on. But maybe it doesn't mean anything. Maybe I'm seeing it for some other reason that has nothing to do with you."

Hayden couldn't believe he was actually feeling disappointed for her. If he didn't watch himself he was going to get caught up in this ridiculous fantasy of hers.

"Is there anything else?" he asked.

"Not really. Other than you."

The mere idea that this woman had seen him in a vision, long before he'd met her, seemed absurd, yet somewhere deep inside him it also felt extremely intimate. Hayden tried not to dwell on that part of it, though. Being connected to this woman physically would no doubt be a pleasure. But a spiritual link was something altogether different.

"What am I doing when you see me?"

"Smiling. In sort of a sexy, taunting way. Like you've known me for a long time and that we were on very familiar terms. Like we didn't need words to understand each other."

Hayden gripped his coffee cup. "You mean, like lovers?"

Claudia nodded with faint embarrassment. Since she'd never made love to a man, it felt awkward for her to express such things to this man. Yet he didn't seem to be embarrassed by her suggestion. "Floored" would have been a better description, she thought as she noted the arch of his dark brows.

"That's exactly what I mean," she murmured, then shook her head in dismay. "It doesn't make sense, Hayden. That's why the whole thing has been so troubling to me."

Disturbed more than he wanted to admit, Hayden said, "Maybe this person only looks like me."

"We've already gone through this theory. I don't know anybody else that resembles you. Is there anyone else in your family that looks like you? A brother?'' she asked.

"I don't have any siblings," he said with a shake of his head, then all of a sudden his eyes grew wide. "Wait a minute. I don't know why I didn't think of this before. There is someone."

Jumping to his feet, he grabbed her by the hand and quickly led her toward the house.

"Who is it? Where are we going?" she asked as they entered the kitchen, then hurried through the living room.

"I have a small office on this end of the house. I want you to look at something there."

The two of them passed through a short hallway. At the end, Hayden opened a door to their left and ushered her inside.

"You didn't explore this room today?" he asked as Claudia looked curiously around the small space.

Shelves were built on three walls, most of which were filled with books and souvenirs that appeared to have been collected on vacations and other special occasions. The remainder of the room was taken up by a large oak desk equipped with a computer, telephone and fax machine.

"No!" she exclaimed. "I haven't been snooping around your house!"

He chuckled. "I wouldn't have cared how much you looked, Claudia. I don't have anything around here I need to keep hidden."

His fingers were still tightly woven through hers and she was stunned at how right it felt to be touching him again, to be connected to him in such a simple but trusting way. He was the man in her visions, not a man she was supposed to allow into her heart.

"You wanted me to look at something?" she murmured, lifting her eyes up to him.

His gaze skittered over her face, then lingered briefly on her lips. "Yeah," he said absently. "It's right over here."

Hayden dropped her hand then, planting his palm against the middle of her back, he guided her to the back wall of the small office. On the middle shelf, he picked up a framed, five-by-seven photo and handed it to her.

"Does this look familiar?" he asked.

Claudia sucked in a harsh breath. Her head began to reel. "Who—Hayden! Who is this?"

"My grandfather. William Hayden Bedford."

Claudia's head swung back and forth in amazement. "But he looks so much like you! He could be your father!"

Hayden chuckled. "He liked to think he was my father. But Dad had a way of reminding him of the chain of command, so to speak."

Gripping the wooden frame, Claudia stared down at the image behind the glass. The man was standing beside a truck with the Bedford Roustabout logo printed on the door. His tall, muscular build was exactly like Hayden's. His rough features could have been taken from the same mold. Even the wave of his dark hair was an identical match. The resemblance was more than uncanny.

"Oh, Hayden, I'm so confused. Now that I see this man, I'm wondering if *he* might be the one in my visions. He looks like him. But then, so do you," she whispered in confusion.

His hands closed over her shoulders. "Are you serious?"

Still clutching the photo, she looked up at him with

troubled eyes. "Yes. I'm— Oh, I don't know. The two of you look too much alike."

"But it makes even less sense for you to be having visions of my grandfather. He's been dead for seven or eight years now."

Outside the sky had darkened and thunder was beginning to rumble ominously in the distance, but Claudia told herself there wasn't any need to be alarmed about the approaching storm. Hayden had already struck her with a lightning bolt.

"I know, Hayden! It doesn't make sense. But what if it is your grandfather that I've been seeing? What could that possibly mean? Dear God, what sort of link could I have to a dead man?"

Chapter Six

Beneath his hands, Hayden could feel Claudia's body begin to tremble. Fear glazed her brown eyes. Releasing his hold on her shoulders, he lifted up her hands to see that she wasn't wearing the opal.

"Where's the ring?" he asked.

"In my bedroom. I don't want to wear it."

"Maybe you should wear it," he said, shocking himself as much as her. "Another vision might give you a few more clues."

Her face was growing pale. Almost as pale as yesterday, when she'd first walked into his office. He led her over to a desk chair and forced her into it.

"Are you worried there might be a tornado coming? I can turn on the weather radio," he said in an effort to comfort her.

Shaking her head, she said, "I'm not worried about the weather! I feel like I've already been hit by a tornado, then fried with lightning." She pushed loose strands of glossy brown hair back from her face, then fixed her gaze on his. "You weren't serious about me wearing the ring, were you? You don't even believe I'm having visions! Much less that they're caused by the ring!"

Hayden rubbed a hand across his forehead. "No, I don't. I don't know what made me say that about the ring. The only thing evident to me is that something strange is going on here."

Just hearing that much of an admission from him brought a sigh of relief rushing past Claudia's lips.

"Hayden, yesterday when I walked into your office, I thought I had this all figured out. I thought you were the man I was searching for! Why didn't you tell me there was someone else in your family that looked like you?"

He shrugged both shoulders. "That thought never entered my mind. Besides," he added, his expression turning sheepish, "I believed you'd traveled down here to south Texas to con me. My grandfather didn't factor into it."

Groaning with disappointment, she closed her eyes and pressed her fingers against the aching lids. "Okay, so it's a possibility I've made a mistake about the man in my vision. If that's true, then we'll have to start over." She opened her eyes to look at him with fresh hope. "Is there any connection that you know of between William Bedford and the house? Or the boat?"

Hayden sat on the edge of the desk so that he was facing her. "I don't know about the house," he said, "but the boat belonged to my grandfather. He purchased it way back in the nineteen forties from someone down on the gulf and renamed it the *Stardust*. After the old song, I think."

Claudia felt a stirring of excitement. "Then maybe it is him I'm seeing," she murmured. "But why?"

"I couldn't say. I only know that he loved to be out on the water. So do I." He picked up a pen and absently rolled it between his palms. "That's why he left the boat to me. Dad never did have any interest in sailing or fishing."

A thoughtful frown settled over her face, then she said abruptly, "I have to go down there, Hayden. I have to see the boat. I think that's the connection I need to put this all together."

For long moments he was quiet, as though he was struggling to absorb her words, then he tossed the pen back onto the desk and quickly rose to his feet. "Claudia, that's crazy. A sailboat can't talk!"

"Don't tell me it's crazy, Hayden," she said tightly. "I've heard that term too much lately."

"All right," he relented gruffly, "then I'll say a trip down to the coast would be pointless." Walking over to the window, he pulled back the curtain and peered out. Tree limbs were bowing beneath the force of the wind. Rain was beginning to spatter the glass panes. The dogs were going to be whining at the back porch, he realized.

"Pointless? Sitting here—"

Angry at himself for letting her be such a distraction, he interrupted. "I've got to go see about the dogs."

Claudia watched him hurry out of the office. Then casting one last glance at the photo of William Bedford, she rose to her feet and went in search of Hayden.

She found him on the back porch urging the dogs to lie down on a dry rug. The animals did as they were told and curled up together, both of them shivering from fear and the sharp drop in temperature.

"Are the dogs okay?" she asked.

Hayden looked up to see her standing a few feet away. A look of concern was on her face and the idea that she actually cared about the dogs touched him. Saundra had hated pets of any kind, saying they were all nasty nuisances. Accepting the black-mouthed curs was one of the first things he'd done after their divorce.

"They'll be fine now. The lightning frightens them."

Claudia went over and kneeled down next to the dogs. As she stroked their damp fur, she murmured comforting words to them. Hayden watched, quietly amazed to see their shivering stop and their eyelids droop. Obviously she had a calming effect on his dogs. But he couldn't say the same for himself. Everything about the woman excited and provoked him.

"You're probably getting cold," he said after a bit. "We should go in."

Claudia rose to a standing position and looked out at the waning storm. "I'm fine. I'm just wondering why you're angry with me."

Hayden closed the few steps between them. "I'm not angry, Claudia."

She turned her head to look up at him. "You sounded that way. Back in the office."

There was something so vulnerable, so desperate, in her brown eyes that he wanted to enfold her in his arms and promise her a rainbow. He wanted to keep her safe from everything and everyone. Including himself.

"I was irritated," he admitted. "I want you to look at things sensibly. Not go running off on a wild-goose chase."

"What does it matter to you?"

Good question, Hayden thought. None of it should matter to him. If she wanted to go look at a hundred sailboats, that was her business. He had a company to run. Three new rigs had just gone up in Guadalupe county last week and they all needed services from Bedford Roustabout. His crews were already stretched thin and it looked as if he was going to have to spend extra time for interviews to hire more hands. He couldn't take care of his job and worry himself with Claudia Westfield's whims at the same time, he told himself.

"Well, it doesn't, I suppose."

She grimaced. "You act like it bothers you that I've shifted my attention to your grandfather rather than you."

His mouth fell open. "That's ridiculous!"

"Is it?" She turned slightly so that her gaze was squarely on his and for a split second as she looked into his blue eyes Claudia felt that she hadn't just met this man yesterday. That she'd known him, loved him, a time long ago. The uncanny sensation sent prickles of awareness dancing down her spine. "I don't believe you're being honest with me."

Irritated by the notion that she could perceive his feelings so clearly, Hayden glanced away from her. "Claudia, you've been swearing all this time that *I* was the man in your visions. It doesn't feel too flattering to be replaced by a ghost."

Shaking her head, Claudia rested her palms against his chest. Her voice softened as she tried to explain. "I'm not seeing a ghost, Hayden. The man I see is flesh and blood, like you. I'm just not completely sure it's your face."

He ought to feel relieved, but he wasn't. He was jealous, damn it! Of a vision! If that wasn't enough to scare him, then the desire that was quickly heating his body should be ringing alarm bells.

"I don't want you to go to Port O'Connor," he said firmly.

His abrupt statement jolted her. "Why? I'm only going to look at the boat. I won't disturb anything," she promised.

"I'm not worried about the boat, Claudia."

The warmth of his body beckoned to her and before she realized what she was doing, her hands had slid up to his shoulders and her breasts were pressed against his chest.

"Then what's the problem?"

The huskily murmured question was as much of a provocation as the feel of her soft curves melting into him. Hayden didn't let himself think beyond the moment, he brought his hands up to her waist and pulled her even closer.

"I'm worried about you," he said lowly. "About this whole thing. I think you should forget it. *We* should forget it."

The urge to raise up on tiptoes and touch her mouth to his was throbbing inside her like an insistent drumbeat. She tried to push the craving to one side of her mind as she whispered thickly, "Why? Because you're afraid you'll find out that I've been telling the truth?"

His hands slid slowly upward, along her rib cage. Another inch and the weight of her breasts would be riding his thumbs. "No. Because it's folly. It's unwise. It's making the two of us act strange."

"Strange?" She sounded breathless and totally unlike herself.

"Yeah," he said regretfully as his eyes devoured the soft features tilted up at him. "Like this. I've already had one woman in my life, Claudia, and that was enough. I don't want to get tangled up again. I don't need that kind of pain.''

Anger pushed away the hazy veil of desire from her mind. ''And you think I do? For the past two years I've been afraid to look at a man. Much less touch one! Do you honestly think I came here just to seduce you?''

Even if she hadn't, she was doing a dandy job of it, anyway, Hayden thought ruefully.

''No. I don't necessarily think you set out to make me want you. But—''

Claudia twisted out of his arms and turned her back on him. Her breaths were coming and going in rapid succession. Her heart was thudding at a sickening pace. ''The only thing I set out to do was unravel the mystery of my visions. As for making you want me...I don't think you do. I mean, it's not actually me you're wanting. I just happen to be close and handy.''

Suddenly his hands were gripping her shoulders from behind. ''That's a nasty thing to say. My secretary is close and handy, too. But that doesn't mean I want to kiss her every time I look at her.''

He wanted to kiss her that much? she wondered wildly. Just the idea thrilled her. But she couldn't let herself believe such a thing. Trusting Tony, then discovering he was a liar had nearly crushed her. Putting any sort of faith into Hayden's words would be asking to be hurt all over again.

''I'm sure she'll be disappointed to hear that.''

He gave her a little shake. ''I wish to hell Lottie had never allowed you into my office.''

Pain that she couldn't understand suddenly filled her heart. ''And I wish I'd never stepped inside it, either!''

As soon as the words were out, she regretted them. Bending her head, she covered her face with both hands.

"That isn't true, Hayden," she said, her voice strained. "I'm glad I found you. I was *supposed* to find you."

For a moment her declaration stunned him, then slowly he turned her around to face him. "Why? Because of that damned ring?"

"Something led me this far," she reasoned. "That's why I can't stop now. I'm going to see the boat. Hopefully something about it will settle my troubled mind. And afterward—well…" She focused her eyes on the middle of his chest. "No matter what happens, you'll probably never have to see me again."

He groaned. "And that's supposed to make me happy?"

"It should. You just told me you don't want another woman in your life. I'm trying to assure you that I won't be hanging around to mess up your plans."

She was right. He should be happy. But just the mere idea of never seeing Claudia again made his future seem dead and pointless. What was happening to him? Falling in love with a woman took more than forty-eight hours. Besides, he wasn't falling in love, he mentally argued. He was just infatuated with her and the whole strangeness of the situation.

"All right," he said, "if you just have to go see the boat, then I'll go with you."

Shaking her head, Claudia quickly pulled away from his hold. "No. I don't think that would be a good idea, Hayden. I'll rent a car and drive myself."

"It's a hundred and forty miles or so to Port O'Connor. I don't want you driving that far alone."

She countered his excuse with a soft laugh. "I've driven much farther than that all by myself. I'm a big girl, Hayden. And if I have any breakdowns I have a cell phone."

"Damn the cell phone," he cursed.

Feeling certain that she was losing ground with him, Claudia edged past him and into the house. Hayden followed quickly on her heels.

"You're not my keeper, Hayden Bedford. And anyway," she said as he continued to dog her heels into the living room, "you have a job you have to take care of."

"It won't fall apart without me for a day or two."

Yes, but would she fall apart with him? she wondered. Two days hadn't yet passed and she was already envisioning making love to the man! He was turning her into an impulsive, reckless wanton! The best thing she could do now would be to get the trip over with as quickly as possible then head home to Fort Worth.

"Okay," she said with a sigh of surrender. "I can see there's not much point in arguing with you about this. When do you want to leave?"

"Right after breakfast."

She nodded. "I'll be ready," she said with a nod, then turned and started out of the room.

"Where are you going now?" he called after her.

Pausing, she looked over her shoulder at him. "To bed."

"At eight-thirty!"

"I think we've had enough of each other's company for one evening, don't you?"

No, Hayden thought. He wanted to lead her back outside into the damp, rain-cooled evening. He wanted to sit beside her on the porch swing, slide his arm around her shoulders and bend his face to the clean flowery scent of her hair. It wouldn't matter if she said a word. It wouldn't matter if he said a word. Just as long as she was close to him. But why tempt matters when he knew he was going to have to let her go soon? he asked himself. Why make more memories than his heart could bear to remember?

"I suppose we have, Claudia. Good night."

"Good night," she replied, then forced herself to leave the room before she could change her mind and run straight into his arms.

"Lottie, I know what the hell I'm doing! Tell Vince to go out to rig 45 and make sure the generators are all set up. The water line should already be down and pumping. Yes, they're buying water off a landowner's pond for right now. We've already set the pump. Lottie, if the pond goes dry it'll be the drilling company's problem, not mine. No, I won't be back by this evening. Tomorrow, probably. You have my pager number and my cell number if you need me. In the meantime, don't worry. No, damn it, I'm not running off to get married! How could you think such a thing after Saundra? Well, then you know something I don't!"

Hayden put down the phone before his secretary could say any more, then turned to refill his coffee cup. It was then he noticed Claudia standing just inside the kitchen. She was wearing a white dress printed with red tropical flowers. The top fit snugly around her breasts and waist while the skirt fluttered around her tanned calves. A tentative smile tilted her lips and as she walked toward him, something jolted in the region of his heart.

"Good morning," he said.

"Good morning," she returned his greeting. "Sounds like this trip is already causing you trouble."

She didn't need to know just how much, Hayden thought. If she did, she might get to thinking she was getting special attention from him. And that wasn't the case. He wasn't going to give any woman special attention. Even one as beautiful and intriguing as Claudia.

"I was just juggling a few things with my secretary," he explained. "Would you like to eat before we leave or stop and have breakfast on the way?"

"Breakfast on the way sounds nice," she told him. "Just let me get my bags and I'll be ready."

It wasn't until they were in Hayden's posh Lincoln, heading down Highway 181 that he noticed Claudia was wearing the opal. The sight of it on her hand took him by complete surprise. Especially after she'd vehemently threatened to throw it away on several occasions.

"You're wearing the ring," he said. "I thought you didn't ever want to put it on again."

Shrugging, she said, "I didn't. But I thought about your suggestion and decided you were right. Another vision might help. Now that I've seen a photo of your grandfather, I might be able to distinguish the differences between the two of you. Not that there was any contrast that I could see."

"William was fifty-three in that photo. I'm only thirty-one. That's a big difference."

She turned her head to study his rugged profile and tried not to look at him as a woman but as a detective on a search for clues. "That part of it doesn't matter. The man I see is young. Even younger than you are now, I think."

Each time Hayden had convinced himself this woman had to be lying or even innocently confused about the visions, she said something to put a chink in his doubts.

"Then you believe that you're seeing either him or me in the past?"

Her forehead wrinkled as she considered his question.

"I hadn't really thought about it before, but yes. That must be what I'm doing."

"Then I'll give you a hint. I wore my hair much longer than this when I was in my twenties and my front tooth is slightly lapped over the other one. See?"

He spread his top lip upward in a way to expose more of his teeth. Claudia leaned forward for a closer inspection then laughed at the absurdity of their behavior.

"I don't know whether to feel like a dentist or an idiot," she said, then her laughter sobered. "But if your hints are correct, then I have to conclude that your grandfather is the man I've been seeing all this time."

Once again Hayden felt as if she'd let the air out of him. Which was ridiculous. This wasn't some sort of romantic fantasy thing with her. And even if it was, he didn't need to be a part of it.

"That's odd, Claudia. Really odd."

Turning her head, she stared out the window at the passing landscape. They were traveling through an area where there was nothing but mesquite, prickly pear, grass and cattle. It was lonely, yet she couldn't deny the wild beauty of the land any more than she could deny her growing feelings for the man beside her. More than anything she wanted Hayden to believe in her. But he was a man who wanted concrete proof. His heart would never be capable of simply trusting her and her word.

"I don't understand it any more than you do, Hayden."

"But my grandfather," he protested. "Even if I did believe the ring had some sort of power, why would it be connected to him?"

"You tell me," Claudia said glumly. "If we had that answer we could probably solve this whole riddle."

Chapter Seven

At Floresville they stopped for a leisurely breakfast. Claudia ate *rancho huevos* and downed the heat of the peppers with several cups of coffee. The food helped her recover some of the energy she'd lost from lack of sleep and by the time they rolled into the tiny gulf town of Port O'Connor, excitement began to envelop her once again.

After a five-minute stop at a convenience store for rest room facilities and to fill an ice chest with drinks and food for lunch, Hayden drove to the harbor where the *Stardust* was docked. Along the way, they passed through a residential area full of beach houses, some huge and elaborate, others small and cozy. Mexican fan trees and Sago palms dotted the lawns and bordered the quiet streets, while bougainvillea, hibiscus and oleander flowered in abundance.

With each block they passed Claudia's excitement grew. The white house she'd envisioned had to be close. She could feel it.

"Are you sure there isn't a big white house in this town?" she asked as Hayden braked to a halt behind a stop sign.

"I'm sure there are big white houses in this town, but I don't recall seeing any like you described. We'll tour the place after you look at the boat, okay?"

She nodded. "Yes. I want to see the boat first. I feel like it's more important anyway."

He turned right and headed down a street that ran parallel to an inner canal where covered boat docks jutted out over the water at regular intervals.

After parking the car in an out-of-the-way area, he took Claudia by the hand and led her down a grassy slope, then onto a boarded walkway. The air was hot and heavy with the moisture from the salty sea. Overhead, laughing gulls screeched and swooped above the water while the faint scent of fish and shrimp was carried along on the stiff southeasterly breeze.

The wind whipped at her skirt and tossed it straight up at her face. Laughing, she caught it with her free hand. "You should have warned me to wear shorts like you," she said.

"And missed seeing you in that pretty dress? I'm glad I didn't," he told her. "But if you'd like to change in the cabin of the boat, you can."

Even though his compliment filled her with pleasure, Claudia knew it would be easier to explore the boat without having to worry about the hem of her dress flying over her head. She glanced hesitantly back over her shoulder. "The extra things I brought with me are in my bag in the car. If I change, I'll have to go back after it."

"I will," he offered quickly. He set the ice chest with their food down on the dock next to her feet. "Wait right here and I won't be gone but a minute."

He returned in a matter of moments with her bag and they continued on down the wooden dock. At the third from the last slip, Hayden stopped and pointed to a boat suspended above the water with ropes and other devices.

"There she is," he said. "That's the *Stardust*. Look anything like you thought? Or is that a stupid question?"

Eerily, she stepped forward and peered at the thirty-foot sailboat. "It's exactly like my vision. I can't believe it," she whispered wondrously. "I'm not sure I want to believe it."

The awestruck look on her face bothered Hayden. The best actress in the world couldn't have conjured such a baffled expression.

Taking her by the arm, he moved her to the side of the wooden pier. "Stand here and I'll let the boat down so that we can go aboard. That is what you want, isn't it?"

She looked at him and swallowed as a ball of unexplained emotion knotted her throat. "Oh, yes! If it isn't too much trouble."

He smiled wryly. "After a hundred-and-fifty-mile drive I don't think it would be too much trouble. We might even take her out for a sail." He glanced up at the sky. "If the weather checks out."

Her eyes sparkled with excitement. "I'd like that."

"Do you get seasick? Or do you know?"

"I've been on the ocean before. It never bothered me."

"Good. I don't want a sick woman on my hands."

From what he'd said last night, he didn't want any sort of woman on his hands. But Claudia didn't remind him of that. So far the day had been pleasant and she wanted their time together on the boat to be special.

In a matter of minutes the craft was bobbing on top

of the water and Hayden was helping Claudia onto the shallow deck.

"Why don't you go below and change your clothes before I untie the moorings," he suggested. "It will be rougher once we get out on open water and away from the shelter of the pier."

"I'll be quick," she promised.

The back part of the cabin contained a minuscule bathroom, two small bunks, a tiny built-in table and a few shelves for storage. Claudia didn't attempt to change in the close quarters of the bathroom. Instead, she closed the door that separated the living quarters from the captain's deck and quickly shed her dress.

As she dug a white peasant blouse and a pair of jean shorts from her bag, she could hear Hayden tuning in a weather frequency on a broadband radio. Just knowing he was a few steps outside the door made her acutely aware of her nakedness and she wondered what he would think if he saw her like this with only a triangle of lace for a pair of panties and a bra that struggled to cover her nipples. It was not the sort of underwear he would probably associate with a practical science teacher, but then it would take more than sexy underwear to excite a man such as Hayden. He might find her body totally lacking, she thought as she glanced down at herself.

What was she doing? she silently yelled at herself. She wasn't on this boat to get naked and seduce Hayden Bedford! What was putting these erotic notions in her head? The ring?

Maybe, she thought grimly. And just maybe it was the man himself.

With that unsettling notion in mind, she quickly finished dressing and then fastened her hair into a ponytail with a white silk scarf. When she opened the door, she found him a few steps away at the wheel.

He grinned as she came to stand beside him. "Well, you look like you're ready for a bit of wind and sea now," he said as his eyes traveled down her long, tanned legs. "I wondered what a science teacher's legs looked like. I'm disappointed."

"Really?" she asked stiffly, while thinking he must have been reading her mind while she was dressing.

"Yeah. I was expecting to see a pair of knobby knees and skinny thighs. Maybe a few spider veins from all those hours spent at the blackboard. Your legs are too pretty to belong to a science teacher. And I don't think they go barefoot, either. Too sensible for that."

Claudia rolled her eyes. "I didn't know you were a flirt and a liar."

He feigned an offended look. "I'm neither."

"Then you're blind. I'm not sure if I can trust you to handle this boat," she teased.

"Oh, I think I can see well enough to get us out in the bay." He turned a key on the instrument panel and somewhere far below the deck a motor rumbled to life. "After that, I'll let you handle things."

Laughter rolled past her lips. "Not me, Captain Bedford. I've never driven a boat of any kind in my life. You'll just have to put on a pair of eyeglasses."

Grinning now, he motioned toward a cushioned seating area just behind them. "Have a seat and I'll do my best to keep you safe."

She did as he suggested and he began to inch the *Stardust* slowly out from the dock. Moments later they were in the canal, heading west. To their right, fishing and freight businesses lined the shore. To the left, cattle grazed a small strip of land that separated the canal from the open waters.

For the next few minutes they chugged their way slowly up the canal past a couple of shrimp boats and several smaller fishing vessels. Then a break in the land appeared and a buoy with a number marked the opening in the canal.

Hayden turned through it and headed the *Stardust* south toward gulf waters.

After a few minutes he looked over his shoulder and smiled at her. "What do you think?" he asked.

He was a man doing what he loved the most, she thought. Smiling back at him, she said, "I'm enthralled. It's so beautiful. The water and birds. All the different boats. Is this where you and your grandfather used to sail together?"

"We've been all over this area. That's what I miss the most now that he's gone. I have to do this without him."

Claudia went to stand beside him. As she watched the wind toss his dark hair across his forehead, she asked, "What about your ex-wife? Didn't she like to go boating?"

He shook his head. "Hated it with a passion. As soon as we'd drop anchor she'd start throwing up. She just didn't have sea legs. Besides, she had other interests. Of which I learned about later on," he added grimly.

Compelled to comfort him, Claudia placed a hand on his upper arm. "That wasn't your fault that she had affairs, Hayden."

His mouth twisted. "How do you know? You don't know what sort of husband I was. I must have been lacking somewhere."

The bitter guilt she heard in his voice matched the

same dark feeling that sometimes came over her whenever she allowed herself to think of Tony. For a long time after their relationship had ended, she'd wondered what was wrong with her that he should want other women. Maybe she'd been too thin or too fat. If she'd worn her hair or make-up differently that might have made the difference.... Or maybe it had been her personality. She hadn't smiled or laughed enough, talked enough or about the right things.

"Believe me, Hayden, after my ordeal with Tony I didn't think there was anything right with me. I began to doubt my ability to communicate with people. I felt like I should change everything about my looks. I even considered having my breasts augmented because I thought if I wasn't sexy enough for Tony, then I wouldn't be for any other man."

Shaking his head with dismay, he reached over and brushed his knuckles against her cheek. "He must have done a real job on you, Claudia."

His hand was warm against her face and a rush of tender emotions misted her eyes. "It's not something I'm proud to admit. Like I said before, being deceived by someone you care about is humiliating. That's why I understand about Saundra."

A grimace twisted his lips. "Yeah. I guess you do," he said quietly. "But you weren't intimate with this guy of yours. It was my spouse—the woman I slept with... lived with. That cuts deep, Claudia."

Yes, the more a person loved, the more they were apt to hurt, she thought sadly. Hayden had said he was glad to be rid of Saundra, but he must have obviously loved her a great deal at one time or their breakup wouldn't still be affecting him this much. The idea filled her with envy and regret.

"One of these days you'll realize that Saundra was the one that was lacking. Something on the inside where it really counts. Not you."

He turned his attention back to steering the boat, then after a minute he said, "I'm not so sure you've realized this Tony of yours was a bum steer. Otherwise you would have probably already been married."

Dropping her hand away from his arm, she stuffed both fists into the pockets of her shorts. "I'll marry— someday—when I find the right man."

His gaze remained fixed on the waters beyond the bow of the *Stardust*. "And in the meantime you're going to let that ring of your grandmother's lead you around like a seeing-eye dog."

"I'm not blind, Hayden. Nor am I crazy! Somehow I'm going to make you see that!" she promised hotly, then yelped in surprise as his arm suddenly snaked around her waist and jerked her body into his.

"If that's your intention, then you can do it right now," he muttered roughly.

Baffled by his behavior, she jerked off her sunglasses and studied his face. "What are you talking about?"

He cut the motor to an idle and they began to drift with the waves. "The ring. Throw it overboard and forget the visions," he dared. "We'll start over. Just man to woman. And we'll see what happens from there."

His challenge both thrilled her and frightened her. There was no doubt that she was drawn to him, that she was beginning to feel things for him that she'd never felt for any man before. But was it because of the ring or because she was simply falling in love? she wondered desperately. And if he turned out to be the wrong man, then she'd have nothing to blame but her own faulty judgment.

The struggle between her head and her heart filled her eyes with agony. "If I throw the opal away now, we might not ever solve its mystery."

Disappointment sharpened his features and his voice. "I was right about you all along. You're using the ring as a shield. You're afraid to trust me or any man."

"Maybe," she whispered miserably. "But there might be something to the ring. My grandmother could have been right about it having romantic powers."

"Hell," he cursed mockingly. "You go ahead and believe in that romance-and-love-in-the-clouds stuff, but I've learned better. The only thing that exists between a man and a woman is this."

In stunned fascination, she watched his face dip downward and then she moaned as his lips fastened roughly over hers. The taste of his kiss sent hot desire sweeping through her body like a raging wildfire and made resisting impossible. Her hands, which were caught between the sudden crush of their bodies, managed to crawl up his chest, then fasten at the back of his neck.

The buffeting sea breeze rocked the boat and their bodies tilted. The next thing Claudia knew she was sprawled at an angle on the ledge of cushions and Hayden was on his knees beside her.

With his hands framing her face, he said between heavy breaths, "You see what I mean. This is the real power between a man and a woman."

It was powerful, Claudia thought. So powerful that she wanted to pull him down to her, to feel the weight of his body pressing into her, to feel the smoothness of his heated skin and to taste the wild pleasure of his kisses. She wanted all of that and more. Much more than he was willing to give. "This is lust, Hayden."

His hands quickly slipped to the mounds of her breasts

and as he cupped their weight in his palms, he whispered raggedly, "At least we can see it, feel it. We know it's real."

Her head twisted back and forth against the cushion as pain fell like a heavy weight inside her. "Love is like that, too, Hayden. Only it lives in our heart."

A harsh expression suddenly tightened his features. "You don't believe that any more than I do."

"You're wrong, Hayden! Wrong!"

He ducked his head to kiss her once again, but Claudia rolled away from him and scrambled to her feet.

"Claudia—"

He reached for her arm, but she scurried through the door leading into the sleeping quarters, then slammed it closed between them.

Slowly, Hayden rose to his feet and stared around him in stunned fascination. What in hell had come over him? he wondered. One minute the two of them had been talking and the next thing he knew he'd been gripped with a violent urge to take Claudia in his arms and make love to her. Not lust, but love.

Now that she was out of his sight, he could admit that much to himself. But not to her. No, he'd gone to extremes to make her believe that all he wanted from her was a romp between sweaty sheets. He'd wanted her to think he was incapable of loving. Because he was scared. He was terrified to think of giving his heart again and having it wrung into painful little knots.

Cursing under his breath, he went to the wheel and opened the throttle. Immediately the *Stardust* began to push south into the rolling waves of the gulf.

Inside the cabin, Claudia sank shakily onto one of the beds and pressed her palms against her hot cheeks. She still wasn't quite sure what had happened between her and Hayden. Once he'd started kissing her, she'd been engulfed with desire, swept away to a place where nothing mattered except being next to him.

But then he'd started talking and his words had doused her like a cold rain. He didn't believe in love. He didn't want love. All he wanted from her was sex. Just like Tony.

Groaning, she looked down at the opal on her hand. The ring had led her in the wrong direction! Again!

Oh, Gran, you didn't give me a gift of love. This is a curse. A curse I can't deal with anymore.

With sudden decision, she rose to her feet. There wasn't any point in delaying the inevitable. She was going to tell Hayden to head the *Stardust* back to Port O'Connor, that she was giving up on the ring, and any hopes of ever making any sense of her visions. And perhaps, most of all, she was giving up on him.

Claudia reached for the door, but before her hand could close around the knob a violent wave of dizziness came over her and she reached blindly to steady herself.

As her hand came in contact with the wall, the contents of the tiny cabin seemed to recede into the background. There was a man standing in front of her. He was tall and muscular and he looked like Hayden. But now that she knew the difference, she could see that the man was his grandfather, William. He appeared to be somewhere in his early twenties and was dressed in a tan khaki shirt and matching trousers. Something bright and shiny glowed from each corner of his collar.

"What do you want?" she whispered desperately. "What are you trying to tell me?"

The man didn't answer. But then Claudia didn't really expect him to. Her visions had never spoken before;

there was nothing different to indicate he would now.
Yet she felt as though he was trying to tell her something
through his eyes and the wistful smile on his face.

"What is it?" she called to him. "What *is* it?"

"Claudia! Are you all right in there?"

It took her a moment to realize the voice she heard
belonged to Hayden, but by then she wasn't capable of
answering. She was trembling from head to toe and a
heavy sheen of sweat covered her face and chest. Her
head was swimming and she was half afraid she was
going to throw up.

"Answer me, Claudia."

The door swung open and Hayden managed to catch
her just as she was pitching forward.

"Claudia! What's wrong?" Carefully, he eased her
down onto one of the bunks. "Are you getting seasick?"

"No," she said on a groan, then weakly lifted a hand
to her damp forehead. "Oh, dear Lord, I had another
vision!"

Quickly he pulled out a handkerchief and after pushing her hand away, mopped at the sweat trickling down
her face. "Tell me," he ordered.

"No! It doesn't matter. You don't believe me anyway," she countered in a shaky voice. "Just go. Turn
the boat around and take me home. That's all I want out
of you."

He looked at her for a moment, then walked out of
the cabin. Claudia expected to feel a sudden about-face
in the boat's direction, but instead she heard the motor
die and then the rattle of chain as he lowered an anchor.

Desperately, she pushed herself to a sitting position
and tried to shake away the spinning sensation in her
head.

"Here, drink some of this. You look like you need it."

She looked up to see Hayden thrusting a long-necked bottle of beer at her.

"My head is already whirling," she argued. "I don't need alcohol."

"It's cold and wet and bracing," he said. "Drink it."

Claudia did as he ordered and after several swallows she began to feel a little closer to normal.

"Thank you," she said finally. "I'm better now. You can go ahead and start home."

Soberly he continued to study her. "Home, as in my place? Or are you meaning Fort Worth?"

Tears of anger and despair clawed at the backs of her eyes, but she fought them off. She'd already shown this man too much of her weak side.

"Fort Worth! I want to forget that I ever knew you. I don't want to think about your grandfather or anything else associated with you."

He eased down beside her on the small bunk bed. "All right," he gently agreed. "I'll get you back to my place tonight and you can catch a plane to Forth Worth in the morning. But first I want to hear about this vision."

"I'm not in the mood to be patronized," she muttered stiffly.

Catching her chin between his fingers, he turned her face to his. "You came on this boat to try to learn something. Now isn't the time to fall apart!"

The sternness of his voice got through to her and she took in a deep breath and straightened her shoulders.

"You're right," she said, twisting the cold beer bottle between her hands. "I owe you that much at least."

"You don't owe me anything." He took the bottle

from her and placed it in a holder on a nearby wall. "Just tell me what happened."

She shook her head as though she still couldn't quite settle it all in her mind. "I had decided to tell you to take me home, that I wanted to forget this whole thing about the ring. I started to leave the cabin, but when I reached for the door handle, your grandfather was suddenly standing in front of me."

Hayden's expression was instantly skeptical. "How do you know it was him this time? You were confused before."

She nodded. "That's true. But I know the differences between the two of you now. It was him. He was wearing a khaki uniform of some sort. And there was something shiny pinned to the points of his collar. Silver birds maybe. Or something with wings."

If she'd reached out and slapped him, he couldn't have looked more shocked. The color drained from his face so abruptly that for a moment she wondered if he was becoming ill.

"Hayden? Are you getting sick on me now?"

"No. I—" He shook his head, then in an awed whisper, he said, "Those were wings you saw on William's shirt. Silver wings."

Wide-eyed, she stared at him. "What sort of silver wings? How do you know?"

He reached for her hand and enfolded it between the two of his. "My grandfather was a flyer—a pilot in the army air force during World War II."

Chapter Eight

Claudia gripped his fingers as excitement shot through her. "You hadn't told me your grandfather was in the military, Hayden! I couldn't have known that without seeing him in a vision! So now can you believe me?"

"I want to show you something before I answer that," he said. "Do you feel like standing?"

"Yes! I'm fine."

Hayden helped her from the bunk, then led her outside onto the deck, which was gently pitching with the rolling waves. Even though a few clouds were drifting overhead, the evening sunlight was fiercely bright after the dim interior of the cabin. Claudia blinked as she looked around her.

"See that mass of land directly to the south of us?" Hayden asked.

Claudia turned in the direction he was inclining his head. About a quarter mile away was an island of some sort. She could discern a few light-colored buildings grouped together in a small area. Off to the left, a lone pickup truck was traveling east over the open land.

"Yes, I see. What is it?" she asked curiously. "Some sort of stopover for shrimpers or fishermen?"

"No. That's Matagorda Island. It runs for forty miles or so parallel to the coast. It's a Texas state park now. But during World War II and for many years afterward it served as an air base. My grandfather was stationed there. For about a year of his service, I think."

Walking into Hayden's office and finding the man she'd been seeing in her visions had been a shock to Claudia. But that episode didn't compare to the strange swirl of emotions surging through her at this very moment.

"Hayden, I—oh, my, this is all so unbelievable! A few minutes ago in the cabin your grandfather's presence seemed so real I actually tried to talk to him!" She gripped his arm as her eyes widened with wonder. "It has to be this place!"

He rubbed a hand across his furrowed brow. "I have to agree that something odd just happened," he murmured in total dismay.

"Then you do believe me?" she prodded.

Hayden let out a shaky breath. He'd always thought of himself as a levelheaded Joe who dealt in facts and everyday reality. Something like this happened to people who lived in a fantasy world. Yet he couldn't deny that something strange, something far more than coincidence, was going on with Claudia and that damned ring of hers.

"I guess I have to," he conceded. "You obviously didn't know about my grandfather being a pilot and you didn't know about the island."

"You don't sound all that convinced, though," she said with disappointment.

"I'm not—I just can't understand what any of this means. Or how you could have any connection to William Bedford."

She gazed out at the island and tried to imagine what it must have been like nearly sixty years ago. Hayden's grandfather would have been a very young man at that time with his future just beginning. "Was William married at that time?" she asked curiously.

"No. He didn't marry Grandmother until later, after he'd returned from duty in late 1944."

"Did he serve in action overseas?"

"Yes. But I'm not sure exactly where. He never talked much about his military service. I'm not sure if it bothered him to remember or if that time of his life he wanted to keep private. Either way, I never pressed him about it. After all, by the time I came along, he'd already built the roustabout company. Oil and gas was our interest. That and sailing and fishing."

"Have you ever visited the island?" she asked curiously.

"A few times. Those buildings you see are now used by Texas Game and Wildlife rangers that run the park, but years before they were a part of the old barracks that housed the airmen."

"It must have been a small base," Claudia commented. "I don't see that many buildings."

"There used to be more. But some were dismantled when the air base was moved out and I think some might have been washed away by Hurricane Carla in 1962. But the concrete runways are still in surprisingly good shape. There's a whole network of them on the backside of the island. Would you like to sail around to the beach side and go ashore?" he asked.

Yes burned the tip of her tongue, yet the practical side

of her wouldn't release the one word of agreement. With a doubtful expression, she lifted her face up to his. "I'm not so sure it would be smart to spend any more time together than we have to, Hayden."

"What does that mean?" he asked sharply. "What the hell are we doing down here together anyway?"

Heat flared in her cheeks. "We both know what we're *supposed* to be doing. But for some reason we seem to get sidetracked," she said awkwardly.

"If you're talking about the little episode that happened between us earlier, then forget it," he said grimly. "I told you it wouldn't happen again."

"And that's supposed to reassure me? To make me feel good?"

Hayden lifted both arms then let them fall to his sides. "What else do you want from me, Claudia? We're two different people. We don't think alike. We want entirely different things."

She dared to meet his gaze head-on. "Do we?"

His nostrils flared. "You're chasing after a fairy tale and I need the real thing."

Claudia grimaced with disappointment. "The real thing, meaning sex?"

Shrugging, he glanced away from her. "If you want to put it so bluntly, then yes. I won't deny that I want you." He focused his gaze back on hers. "And I think you'd be lying if you said you didn't want me."

She trembled as the truth of his words hit her. "Maybe I do," she said tightly. "But I won't settle for just that. From you or any man."

He snorted mockingly. "Isn't that moralistic thinking rather old-fashioned? We're two adults with basic human wants and needs. What would be wrong about giving in to them?"

It wouldn't be all that wrong, Claudia thought. If he loved her. But that would never be the case.

She moved a few steps away from him and lifted her face to the cooling sea breeze. She needed to clear her senses, to brace herself against the temptation he was offering her.

"That's fine for some people, Hayden. But not for me. I want to make *love*. Not simply have sex. I want to have an emotional and spiritual connection with the man I give myself to. And if it takes years to find him, then I guess I'll just have to wait."

As Hayden stood there admiring her lovely profile, he realized she was the sort of woman he'd once wanted for a wife, the sort of woman he'd searched for before he'd stumbled onto Saundra. Maybe things would have been different if he'd met Claudia first. But the past was done and his heart couldn't see past the scars around it.

"Like I said before, we have different wants, Claudia."

Her heart heavy, she watched him move to the mast and begin to untie the sails.

"What are you doing?" she asked.

"Putting up the sails. We're going to the other side of the island. If nothing else, we can eat our lunch on the beach."

Claudia didn't argue. They had to eat lunch somewhere and being here on the boat with him was just as tempting as being on an isolated island, she supposed. And who knew, if she was lucky, maybe William Bedford would come to her again and explain just what in the heck he wanted from her.

Since Claudia knew nothing about sailing a boat, she sat out of the way on the deck while Hayden finished his task with the sails, pulled up anchor, then steered the *Stardust* to the east.

Thirty minutes later they rounded the corner of the island. Here the wind was even brisker and the rolling surf of the gulf was breaking onto wide, sandy beaches. Gulls swooped and laughed while brown pelicans skimmed above the water, then nose-dived for unsuspecting fish.

For as far as she could see, the beach was deserted and the only activity she could find on the ocean was a freighter steaming along in the far distance. Claudia got the feeling they'd traveled to another world.

"The water is too shallow to get any closer," Hayden told her as he began to pull in the sails. "I'll have to drop anchor here. Can you wade to shore?"

Claudia pushed herself to her feet. "Of course. I love the water. Do I need to keep my shoes on or pull them off?"

He eyed her canvas pull-ons. "If you don't mind wearing soggy shoes, leave them on. Just be sure and shuffle your feet. That way if you step in the path of a stingray he'll scoot out of your way instead of stabbing you."

"Are there sharks in these waters?"

"Sure there are. But only the babies get this close to shore."

"Do they bite?"

Chuckling, he lifted the foam chest and climbed onto the deck. "Don't worry, Claudia. I wouldn't let anything bite one of those pretty legs of yours. Unless it was me."

Coming from any other man, she would have simply laughed. But from Hayden, the baited remark stuck her like a red-hot poker.

"Hayden, you promised—"

"Oh, hell, Claudia, calm down. I'm not about to start nibbling on your thigh instead of my sandwich. Even though it would probably be tastier."

A pent-up breath suddenly drained out of her and she suddenly wondered why this man had the power to make her feel like a foolish teenager. For Pete's sake, she was twenty-three years old! She'd dated several men in college and then there'd been Tony. It wasn't as if this was the first time she'd been alone with a man.

But not one like Hayden Bedford.

Doing her best to ignore that last thought, she said, "I'm sorry, Hayden, for being so edgy. It's not my plan to make us both miserable. Really."

The wan smile he cast her was both understanding and regretful. "I know, Claudia. Forget it. Let's go enjoy our lunch."

Moments later as they waded to shore, Claudia was glad she'd decided to remove her shoes. The water was extremely warm and the sand as soft as a baby's blanket. Even after they found a spot to sit, she set her shoes aside and delighted in digging her toes into the hot, loose sand.

"It's hard to believe this place was once an air base. Supplies, equipment, everything would've had to have been ferried over from the mainland. What did they use for fresh water?" she wondered out loud.

Hayden handed her one of the sandwiches from the ice chest. "I'm not sure. Obviously, there's a few sources of fresh water on the island because it inhabits lots of wildlife. Even alligators." He motioned with his head toward the grassy dunes a few feet behind them. "Don't wander into the dunes," he warned. "Rattlesnakes are plentiful around here. Not to mention fire ants."

Smiling ruefully, Claudia unwrapped cellophane from a tuna sandwich. "Stingrays, sharks, jelly fish, alligators, fire ants and rattlesnakes. Everything around here will either bite, sting or kill you."

"That's true," he agreed as he gazed out at the endless gulf water. "But it's wild and beautiful, don't you think?"

Yes, it was wild and beautiful. Dangerous and uncontrollable. Just like the feelings she had for him, Claudia thought.

"Very," she agreed. "I'm glad we came here."

"You're not too hot?"

The sun was still a fierce ball in the western sky, but the stiff sea breeze kept the heat from being unbearable. "No. This is lovely."

"Good. I was worried about you earlier. Back on the boat after you'd...had that vision." He'd been more than worried, Hayden realized. When he'd opened the cabin door to see her falling straight toward him, he'd been terrified. Her white face had been glazed with a sickly sheen and for a moment he thought she was going to lose consciousness, maybe even her breath. In that instant he realized just how much he was beginning to care for this woman, how bleak it would be to never see her face or to hear her voice again.

Feeling his eyes moving over her, she turned her head slightly to look at him. The sincerity she found on his face touched her even more than his words. "You shouldn't have been. I get dizzy and sweaty and strange sensations zing through my head. But thankfully it passes quickly."

He took a long drink of bottled water, then tossed a couple of crumbs from his sandwich out to a pair of gulls strutting along the damp shoreline. "Claudia, I want to apologize to you for my behavior back on the boat. I—"

"Hayden, please. Let's just forget it—"

"No. I can't forget it," he interrupted. "Actually, I'm still trying to figure out what came over me. I'm not even sure I remember everything I said to you."

She lowered the sandwich to her lap and stared at him. "You wanted me to throw the ring away. Is that the way you still feel?"

Leaning back on one elbow, he shot her a pained look, then glanced toward the rolling surf. "I don't know what to think about that ring anymore, Claudia. Something is certainly making me act out of character. But I think..."

He paused, then with a rueful groan he scooted close enough to lay his hand on her forearm. "You have a lot more power over me, Claudia, than that damn ring."

"And that bothers you," she said regretfully.

His lips twisted. "A heck of a lot," he admitted. "You're a young, beautiful woman, Claudia. Your future has just begun. You don't need to mix yourself up with a jaded, divorced man. You need someone who believes in rainbows and happy-ever-afters."

The pained look on his features filled her heart with heaviness and she suddenly realized that she could never be happy unless this man beside her was happy, too. The thought was so unexpected, so real, it startled her and for long moments she could say or do nothing. Then finally she reached out and pushed her fingers through the hair at his temple.

"You could believe in those things, too, Hayden. We could believe in them together."

His eyes darkened. Not with anger, but with a fatal kind of sadness. "Not me, Claudia. I guess I'm too dis-illusioned, maybe even afraid to let myself think about having someone to love and share my life with. When you—"

"Hayden, why are you allowing Saundra to crush your spirit this way? If—"

"It's not just Saundra or the divorce, Claudia," he interrupted. "Oh, I'll admit she left a black, ugly spot inside me, but a person can usually wash away a black spot if they scrub hard enough."

Her fingers moved to his cheek. "Then why?"

"It does something to you, Claudia, when you lose your family. Your mother. Father. Wife. Once they were all gone I realized that loving someone was really just a game of chance. You play your cards and you win or lose. I lost. And I just don't have it in me to gamble for happiness a second time."

He couldn't have been more point-blank, Claudia thought. He was telling her straight-out to forget about anything serious ever evolving between the two of them. He was determined to keep his heart to himself. If she was smart she would accept his feelings. But she couldn't. Somehow, some way, he'd become a part of her life. She couldn't just let go. At least not without a fight.

"I thought that way, too, after Tony," she said quietly. "But now, well, things have changed for me."

"I'm glad," he softly replied. "I'm glad that one of us isn't ruined."

Claudia wanted to shout at him that he wasn't *ruined*. She wanted to lean her head into his, to kiss him with her heart and her soul, to give him back all those precious feelings that he'd lost. But instinct told her that too much had already happened between them today. She needed to give him time.

Dropping her hand from his face, she looked away

and took in a steadying breath. "If you're finished eating, I'd like to look around a little. Are there any roads or trails around here that we could walk on?"

Relieved that she'd changed the subject, Hayden rose to a sitting position and fished a couple of sports drinks from the cooler. Handing one of the bottles to her, he said, "About a quarter of a mile on down the beach is a dirt road leading into the island. I'm ready for a hike, if you are."

Twenty minutes later the two of them were standing on a solid concrete runway that stretched for hundreds of yards in an east and west direction. At another point, not far from where they were standing, a second runway crossed in a northeasterly to southwesterly direction. Other than a few clumps of grass and bits of prickly pear pushing up through a few cracks, the airstrips were in perfect condition.

"This is incredible," Claudia exclaimed as she gazed around her in wonder. "It's so eerie and desolate-looking. Yet I can almost see the planes taking off and landing and the activity of the crews on the ground."

"These are only a part of the runways," Hayden informed her. "There're many more as you head over to where the barracks were located."

Claudia wiped her sweat-damp face with the back of her arm. She was hot and tired, but she was glad she'd made the effort to see more of the island. The more she saw, the more convinced she became that the reasons for her visions originated here.

"Hayden, did William ever talk about this place? Or his life while he was stationed here?"

After several swallows from the bottle he was carrying, he said, "Not that I can remember. I'm sure he talked to Dad about it at some time or another. But with Dad being gone, too, that doesn't help matters.''

She glanced up at him. ''I just keep asking myself how this place and your grandfather fits in with my ring.''

Hayden shrugged. ''I've been asking myself the same thing and it doesn't fit as far as I can see. What business would he have had with a woman's opal ring?''

Gloria instinctively touched the ring on her finger as if it could conjure up its own answers. ''Perhaps he bought it for your grandmother? Did he know her then?''

''I don't know all the particulars about how they met or when. But I'm pretty sure they went to the same high school and I do remember Grandmother talking about how she worried like all the other women when their sweethearts went off to war. So apparently the two of them were an item before he left for the military.''

Nodding thoughtfully she said, ''That could account for his having the ring. He must have bought it for your grandmother. But something happened and she never received it. Or maybe she did and sold it later on.''

Hayden shook his head. ''I don't think so. Grandmother was really sentimental. She never sold anything that was given to her as a gift. And I'm dead certain she'd never sell a piece of jewelry that Granddad gave her.''

''Hmm. Neither would Betty Fay,'' Claudia agreed. ''So I guess that rules that theory out.''

''Was the ring new when Betty Fay received it?'' he asked.

Claudia made a helpless, palms-up gesture. ''That's been a question my family has bantered back and forth for years. I think my mother halfway believes Betty Fay purchased the ring at a pawn shop and made up the whole idea about it having romantic powers.''

''Now there's a woman with some sense,'' he muttered.

''Who? Betty Fay or Marsha, my mother?''

He cast her a good-natured frown. ''Marsha. But,'' he added quickly before she could protest, ''that wouldn't account for your visions of William.''

A tiny ray of hope filtered through her. If he could open his mind enough to believe in her visions, then he might be able to open his heart to the future.

''William and the ring are tied together. I'm sure of it,'' she said, then her eyes brightened with another idea. ''What about letters or a journal, Hayden? Surely, William wrote to someone during his stay here. If we could find something like that—''

She broke off as his expression turned futile.

''I'm sorry, Claudia, but if anything like that did exist, it would have burned. My grandparents lost their house to fire back in the eighties. All their personal belongings were destroyed.''

Claudia's heart plummeted. ''Well, so much for that,'' she said glumly.

The disappointment on her face caused an invisible weight to settle on Hayden's shoulders and he had to admit that something in the past two days had changed him. He'd gone from thinking this woman was a fraud to desperately wanting to help her, to make her happy. None of it made sense.

Love doesn't always make sense, Hayden.

The inner voice nearly jerked the ground right from under his feet. He couldn't be falling in love with Claudia! He'd spent most of the afternoon swearing to her that he'd never love again. And he wouldn't. He was wizened, not gullible, he reassured himself. Just because she felt good in his arms didn't mean anything special. She was an attractive female. It was supposed to feel good to kiss her. And as for wanting to make her happy, well he was basically a caring person. He didn't want to see anyone miserable.

Feeling more reassured now that he'd reasoned with himself, he took her by the upper arm and urged her back in the direction of the beach. "Come on, we'd better head to the *Stardust*. The sun will be setting soon and it's a long drive from here to San Antonio."

Especially when you were coming up empty-handed, Claudia thought. But worse than that, this time with Hayden was ending. Tomorrow she would fly back to Fort Worth and try to get her life back to normal. But how could she, when just the idea of never seeing Hayden again was tearing her heart right down the middle?

"Yes, I suppose you're right," she said wistfully. "I only wish—"

She broke off with a strangled cry and grabbed her forehead with one hand.

Instantly, Hayden slipped his arm around the back of her waist. With a hand beneath her chin, he tilted her face up to his. "Claudia! What's wrong? Are you having another vision?"

"I—no. But—" Shaking her head, she tried to focus on his features, but a dark-colored object kept getting in the way. "I'm not sure what's happening. I'm not seeing your grandfather but something is clouding my eyesight," she said frantically.

"The boat? The white house?" he prodded urgently.

"No. No, it's something else." Closing her eyes, she strained to see the object more clearly and by the time she did figure it out, she was weak with shock. "Hayden! There's a book—a diary—something on the boat!"

He stared at her, his expression instantly skeptical. "There can't be. After my grandfather died, I removed everything on the boat that belonged to him."

She clamped both hands around his arms so tightly that her fingers dented his flesh. "Then you must have missed it because it's there! In a dark, hidden place. I'm sure of it, Hayden. We have to look!"

"All right. All right," he said soothingly. "We'll go search, but try not to be disappointed when we come up with nothing."

"Maybe you'd better try not to be too red faced when you have to eat crow," she swiftly countered.

In spite of the heat, the two of them picked up their pace. Fifteen minutes later they were back on the beach, wading to the *Stardust*. After Hayden helped her climb back aboard, he suggested she start searching the sleeping quarters of the cabin while he investigated the area above.

Inside the tiny bedroom, Claudia began to poke under mattresses and drawers while asking herself if she'd gone stark, raving mad. Had she conjured up the image of a diary just out of wishful thinking? And even if they did find such an article, it probably wouldn't be legible after all these years of being near moist saltwater.

In spite of her doubts she continued to examine every crack and crevice in the walls and floors, just in case a board had been loosened enough to slip something beneath it. But after more than an hour of nothing, she left the cabin feeling worse than defeated.

She found Hayden stretched out on his belly peering with a flashlight into the bowels of the boat where the engine sat.

Carefully standing to one side of his shoulder, she asked, "Do you see anything?"

Without bothering to glance up at her, he answered, "Not yet. What about you?"

"Nothing. I must have been seeing wrong. Or perhaps it's not on the boat but some other place your grandfather often visited." She looked toward the west and the huge orange ball sliding toward the watery horizon. "It's going to be dark soon. Maybe we should forget it and head back to the mainland."

"I have one more place to look and then I'll lift anchor," he told her.

Feeling both hopeless and foolish, she watched him hoist a small square in the floor near the helm. "This is where the batteries are stored," he told her. "I've been inside this little cubbyhole dozens of times and I'm sure there's nothing down here except a couple of deep-cell marine batteries. But to give you peace of mind, I'll make sure."

Once again he stretched out on his belly and directed the beam of flashlight into the darkened cavity.

"Is that area walled off or is it a big open space?" she asked curiously.

"I've never tried to figure that out," he answered. "Dark, spidery places aren't usually what a person looks at when he goes sailing."

"All right," she said, trying not to be annoyed by his tart remark. "Just put the lid back and let's go. We're chasing air castles, anyway. I guess I'll do what my mother keeps urging me to do. Go home and see a psychiatrist!"

"Hell," he cursed, his voice partially muffled as he lowered his face into the darkened cavity. "You're not crazy, Claudia. You're just a hopeless romantic."

Confused by his remark, she said, "I told you before that everyone says I'm a cool, practical woman. And the way I remember things that night on your back porch, you wholeheartedly agreed."

He lifted his head long enough to glare at her. "Why is it you women remember every little word a man says to you? I was annoyed that night. I probably said a lot of things. Besides, that was before I got to know you."

The idea that he might be softening tilted her lips into a pleased smile. "You're a good man, Hayden. And I like you even though you don't want me to."

He didn't make any sort of reply and Claudia glimpsed a sheepish expression stealing over his face just before he ducked his head back into the small storage area.

Moving to the helm, Claudia rested her hands on the steering wheel and glanced up at the sky. A handful of clouds in the west were now painted with the pink and purple hues of sunset and pelicans glided peacefully over the water. Everything appeared calm and beautiful. Which made it seem even more odd when a cool chill suddenly raced down her spine. She glanced to the east, half expecting to see a summer squall heading toward them, but the sky was amazingly clear.

"I don't expect you to keep looking, Hayden," she told him. "I can accept being wrong. Forget it. Let's pull up anchor and get out of here. Something doesn't feel right."

"Just a minute. There's one more corner—" His muffled voice trailed off and then he said, "Well, I'll be damned. I think I see something."

Claudia practically jumped to his side. "What is it?"

He raised up to a sitting position. "Can't tell yet. It looks like some sort of box. Could just be an old battery holder or something like that. But it's out of my grasp. I need a tool long enough to reach with.''

Moments later, with the aid of a small fish net, Hayden managed to drag the object close enough to get his hands on. When he pulled the small metal box up onto the deck both he and Claudia stared at it as if they'd just pulled up sunken treasure.

''It's locked!'' Claudia exclaimed.

Hayden jerked on the rusty lock but it didn't budge. ''Well, back in the old days I could have shot it off with a .45, but I guess I'll have to resort to a hacksaw.''

''What do you think it is? Have you ever seen this box before?'' Claudia rushed the questions at him.

''Your guess is as good as mine, Claudia. I've never seen the thing. More than likely there's old fishing lures inside it,'' he said in an effort to play down the suspense. ''William never threw anything like that away.''

He went over to another storage area in the side of the hull and pulled a hacksaw from an assortment of tools he always carried on the *Stardust* in case of emergencies.

''But why lock the thing, then hide it?'' Claudia asked, unable to contain her excitement. ''Are fishing lures that valuable?''

Hayden chuckled. ''That depends on how devoted a fisherman you are.''

Claudia practically held her breath while he sawed through the loop on the lock, then groaned with frustration when he didn't immediately lift the lid.

''What are you doing? Open the darn thing!'' she exclaimed.

He picked up the box and carried it over to the ledge of cushions. ''Come over here where we can sit down together and look at whatever is inside.''

Quickly, Claudia followed and eased down close beside him. Her heart was drumming in her ears and the sensation that a wild wind was about to blow seemed to surround the two of them like an invisible cloak. The impression was so strong it actually frightened her and she grabbed Hayden's arm before he could lift the lid to the box.

"Something is—I don't know, Hayden, maybe we shouldn't open this thing," she whispered fervently.

He looked at her with amazement. "Claudia! You practically begged me to search this boat! We traveled all the way down here from San Antonio because of your hunches. And now that we've found something, *you* don't want to open it!"

Helpless to explain the strange intuitions coming over her, she shook her head. "I'm sorry I'm being so difficult! It's just that maybe it wasn't intended for us to uncover what's hidden inside. Maybe something terrible will happen to us if we do!"

She was trembling now, but whether her case of jitters was from fear or excitement, she wasn't sure. In any case, she was relieved that he didn't laugh at her. Instead, he totally surprised her by putting his arm around her shoulder.

"Claudia," he said as he gently pulled her close to his side, "nothing is going to harm us. We're here together."

Together. Together, forever.

The two words swirled through her like a calming mist and all at once she knew this was exactly as things were meant to be. The two of them here together, finding the box and the revelation inside. Hayden was the man she'd been looking for, Claudia realized with sudden clarity. William might have been the image in her visions, yet he'd only been leading her to the man she would love for the rest of her life.

Now all she had to do was convince Hayden. A man who didn't even believe in rainbows.

Chapter Nine

Moments later Hayden pulled a white plastic bag from the metal container and carefully dumped the contents onto his lap.

Beside him, Claudia sucked in a swift, silent breath as her eyes took in a leather-bound journal along with two bundles of white envelopes tied with blue ribbon.

"Oh, my! Oh, Hayden. Are they—did they belong to your grandfather?"

Totally stunned, Hayden carefully lifted one of the bundles of letters and read the address from the top envelope. "This one is addressed to him. The return is from a woman. Betty Fay Alderson."

Claudia could actually feel the blood draining from her head. Instantly her ears began to ring. Her hands went cold, her heart stopped. "That can't be! That's— Hayden, that's my grandmother's maiden name!"

Hayden felt as if an explosion had suddenly rocked the earth beneath them. In total disbelief, his head swung back and forth. "I can't believe this, but I have to. The evidence is right here in my hands."

"What does this mean?" she whispered frantically. "That they were lovers?"

Still stiff with shock, he handed her a bundle of the letters, then warily opened the journal. Before he began to read, he picked up a faded, dog-eared snapshot that was tucked snugly in the spine between the first two pages. Incredibly, the black-and-white image had been taken of a young, dark-haired woman standing in front of a two-story house such as Claudia had described in her vision.

Handing the photo to her, he said, "Look, Claudia. This is the house you've been hunting. Could that be your grandmother when she was in her early twenties?"

Dazed, Claudia nodded. "Yes. I have a few photos that were taken of her when she was very young." She flipped the snapshot over and read. "Hotel Lafitte. Seadrift, Texas. Nineteen forty-three."

"Where is this?" she asked. "Do you know?"

"Yeah. It's a little fishing town about eighteen miles west of here."

She closed her eyes and groaned. "I suppose that's why I kept getting the feeling the house was close by. I wonder what they were doing there?"

His lips twisted with wry cynicism. "What most other lovers at that time were doing when a soldier had a weekend furlough."

Claudia's face flamed. "I'm not a prude, Hayden. But to think of my grandmother having an affair…" She placed a hand against her chest. "It just knocks the air right out of me."

Though he didn't admit it, Hayden was experiencing the same sort of bewilderment. He wasn't necessarily surprised that William had once had an affair. After all, he'd been a good-looking, virile man up until the day he'd died. And he'd been a man who liked women, though Hayden was always quite certain he'd never cheated on Alice during their marriage. No, the amazing part of this whole thing was that William might have been in love with Claudia's grandmother.

"From the looks of her, she was a beautiful, vibrant woman. I can certainly see why my grandfather would have been drawn to her. But perhaps we'd better read some of this stuff before we draw any more conclusions," he suggested.

Nodding, Claudia untied the ribbon and opened the first letter from the stack. At the same time Hayden turned his attention to the journal.

Some thirty minutes later, twilight had fallen and tears were streaming down Claudia's face. Lifting her head from the letter lying open in her lap, she wiped her eyes with the backs of her hands.

From what she'd read so far, she'd discovered that Betty Fay had been living in Port O'Connor, working at a fish house when she'd met a young soldier named William Bedford. The two had fallen in love instantly and their relationship quickly deepened into a serious affair. So far the letters talked of marriage, but sadly, Claudia knew that a marriage must have never taken place.

"I don't think anyone in the family knew about Betty Fay living down here on the coast. Or maybe they did and I just never heard about it," Claudia said, her voice husky with tears. "I just keep wondering why she never told anyone about William. Why keep it a secret—especially after her husband died?"

"I've been wondering the same thing about my grandfather, Claudia. And the only thing I can figure is that it was just too private and painful to share with anyone. Still, you would have thought the two of them would have gotten together later on, after their spouses passed away.''

"Think about it, Hayden. When Betty Fay's husband died, William's wife was probably still living. And she went on to outlive William herself, didn't she?''

Hayden nodded. "Yes. Grandmother only died about a year ago and she'd become feeble a couple of years before that.''

"It seems the timing was never right for Betty Fay and William to be together." A fresh set of tears burned her eyes and Claudia closed her lids in an effort to ward them off. "In this letter she's talking about their plans to get married after his army duty was over. I wonder what happened back then? I can't believe the two of them simply fell out of love. This wasn't just some frivolous infatuation. The fact that William saved all these letters and Betty Fay cherished the ring tells me that the two of them must have loved each other until the day they died. It's just too sad to think about.''

Torn by her tears, he slipped his arm around her shoulders and tilted her head to the curve of his shoulder. "You're taking all this too hard, Claudia. Their lives are in the past now. It's futile for you to cry over what might have been.''

Sniffing, she lifted her head far enough to study his grim profile. "Surely you're not so unfeeling that this doesn't affect you!''

It had affected him, Hayden realized. Far more than he ever wanted to admit to Claudia or to himself. Especially after reading several entries that William had written in the latter part of the journal.

Somewhere in Europe, during William's military stay,

he'd purchased an opal ring from an old Gypsy woman, who'd insisted the stone was blessed with love. When his tour of duty was finally over, he'd brought the ring back to Betty Fay with every intention of marrying her. But when he'd returned to San Antonio after his military duty, he'd learned that Alice was pregnant. He'd went on to write that since there was a slim possibility the baby could be his, he couldn't shirk his duty to become Alice's husband and the baby's father. But in spite of this, his heart would remain with Betty Fay.

As far as Hayden was concerned the whole story of his grandfather's life was just more solid proof that true love couldn't endure. Real life always got in the way.

He sighed as a heavy weight seemed to settle on his shoulders. "My grandfather spent years agonizing over a woman he couldn't have. You think that doesn't affect me?"

"That's the impression I got," she said quietly, then seeing the ragged look on his face, she groaned with remorse. "I'm sorry, Hayden. I don't know what made me say that. I realize you're not made of iron. It's just that this revelation has jerked at my very roots. And I'm making everything worse by weeping all over you."

He squeezed her hand, then handed her the journal. "Here. Read this. It can explain better than I as to what happened between our grandparents. Right now I'd better get the *Stardust* on its way back to Port O'Connor."

Rising to his feet, he went straight to the upper deck of the boat and began to hoist the sails. Claudia took the letters and the journal into the sleeping quarters. At the table, she lit a fat candle that was anchored by a heavy lead holder, then sat and opened the journal.

Above her, she could hear the creaking deck, the flap

of canvas and Hayden's footsteps. Eventually, the *Stardust* drifted into deeper water and Claudia began to read.

More than an hour and a half later, Hayden entered the cabin to find Claudia still reading. As he took a seat on the edge of one of the bunks she lifted her head and looked at him through bleary eyes.

Closing the journal, she pushed her wind-tangled hair back from her face. "Are we close to Port O'Connor yet?" she asked.

He smiled wanly. "We're already docked."

She glanced around her, amazed that she hadn't noticed the movement of the boat had stopped.

"Oh. I had no idea I'd been in here that long. I guess I was so immersed in your grandfather's writings, I lost all track of time."

"That's understandable. I haven't been able to think about much else." He patted the empty spot at his side. "Come over here," he said softly. "I want to talk to you."

Her heart kicked into a nervous thump as she left the table and sank down next to him. "Are you angry with me?"

The question seemed to take him by surprise. He shifted toward her, his brows arched. "Angry? Why should I be?"

She shrugged and he reached for her hand. After tightly enfolding it in his, he rested them both on his knee.

Guilt shadowed her brown eyes as they swept over his face. "I've disrupted your work, your daily routine, everything. And now it looks like I've managed to demolish the sacred memories you had of your grandfather. I'm sorry, Hayden. That wasn't my intention at all.

When I first came to you in San Antonio I had no idea I was going to eventually uncover something like this.''

He took in a long breath then slowly released it. This woman was too good for him, he realized. There wasn't a selfish bone in her body. Once she had a husband, he would get her complete devotion. And she would deserve the same sort of love and commitment from him. But Hayden had already walked that path and failed. He couldn't be a husband again. He couldn't be what Claudia needed and that fact was like a knife blade in his heart.

"That's what I want to talk to you about. I want to apologize.''

This time the surprise was on Claudia's face. "I think you need to turn that around, Hayden. I'm the one who should be apologizing. You didn't ask for any of this.''

With a shake of his head he said, "I didn't ask for any of it. But that doesn't excuse the fact that I said some awful things to you. I accused you of lying and even worse, trying to pull some sort of con game for money. When all along you were being totally forthright with me. Do you know how much of a heel that makes me feel?''

Soberly, she touched her hand to his cheek. "My own parents doubted my visions. Why should you feel guilty for doubting me?''

Because there was a sweetness, a goodness inside her that he'd not found in Saundra or any other woman he'd known in the past, Hayden thought. That in itself should have been enough to make him see she was genuine. But then, it was as he'd told Claudia before, his heart was too jaded to believe in anything or anyone.

"Well, I do. Because I realize some of what I said

hurt you. And I don't want you going back to Fort Worth thinking I was a total jackass.''

Back to Fort Worth. Just hearing the words filled her heart with lead weight. How could she go back now? she wondered miserably, when her heart would stay here in south Texas with him.

Swallowing at the ache that was building in her throat, she said, ''I wouldn't be thinking anything like that, Hayden. I—''

He watched her gaze drift toward their clasped hands. ''You what?'' he prodded.

Like an earthen dam trying to hold back a raging river, something inside Claudia gave way and she groaned as she was unable to stop the flood of emotions rushing through her. ''Oh, Hayden, can't you see that I've fallen in love with you?''

His head actually reared back as though she'd struck him. ''No!''

The negative reaction stung, but didn't surprise her. ''You just said you believed in me. That you knew I was a truthful person. Why don't you believe me now?''

''I don't think you're lying, Claudia! I just think you're confused. We've only known each other a few days. You couldn't have. This whole thing with the visions and our grandparents' affair has gotten you messed up. You're emotional. Overwrought.''

Desperate to convince him, she shook her head. ''No, Hayden. I realized I loved you before we ever found the journal and the letters. I just didn't say anything. But now, well, I couldn't go back to Fort Worth without letting you know how I felt.''

Releasing her hand, he scraped fingers from both hands though his tousled hair. Misery marked his face as he glanced away from her. ''Look, Claudia, I've already explained to you how I feel about love and marriage. This thinking of yours is only going to make you and me both unhappy.''

Claudia felt as if a big gaping wound had just opened in her chest. ''Hasn't anything that's happened today gotten through to you, Hayden? You tell me you believe in my visions—''

''I have to,'' he interrupted. ''Otherwise, we would have never discovered the journal. As far as that goes, you would have never come to San Antonio looking for me.''

Hope suddenly sparked in her eyes. ''That's right. That's what I'm trying to say. The ring wasn't just leading me on a quest to uncover an affair that happened sixty years ago. It was leading me to you.''

''Oh, hell!'' He jumped to his feet and backed away from her as though she'd just turned into a serpent. ''You don't believe that any more than I do.''

She stood and looked at him with eyes that begged him to open his mind and his heart. ''I believe it with everything inside of me,'' she whispered. ''In Gran's letters, she talks about the opal and how she and William both believe that the ring somehow absorbed the power of their great love. I think they were right. Love is the most powerful thing that exists and the ring proves that the power of such love can transcend all time.''

All he could do was stare at her as she walked forward and slipped her arms around his waist.

''We were meant to be together, Hayden. My grandmother told me if I wore the opal I would find my true love. Now I have.''

Hayden had never felt so cornered or desperate in his entire life. The feel of having Claudia back in his arms was becoming a familiar pleasure. One that he didn't want to give up. Yet she wasn't a woman who would agree to an affair and even if she would, he'd have to refuse. Because he wanted her to be happy. And in the end, love was the only thing that would give her complete happiness.

"Betty Fay didn't give you my name. Besides," he continued to argue, "if we were so destined to be together, why didn't the ring lead you to me in the first place?"

Trying to ignore the pain in her chest, she answered, "No, Betty Fay didn't give me any man's name. And the ring didn't lead me to you first because you were married four years ago. *You* married the *wrong* woman!"

Because he couldn't resist, his hands slid up and down the warm contours of her back. "Claudia, I'll admit that something out of the ordinary has been going on with you—with us. And this thing with the ring leading us to find out about our grandparents affair is, I'll admit, more than coincidental. But none of this means that we're supposed to be in love. Like they were."

His words were like a slap that opened her eyes to the whole picture in front of her and humiliation burned through her like a shot of raw whiskey. She'd been a fool again. Just because she loved the man didn't mean he reciprocated her feelings. Or that he ever would.

"I guess you were right, Hayden. I got a little carried away. And I've put you in an awkward position. Sorry about that. Any smart girl ought to know that her feelings can't always be returned." Unable to hold his gaze, she dropped her head and whispered miserably, "I wasn't thinking. I had this naive notion that if you knew that I loved you then you would automatically love me back." She laughed in an effort to hide her pain and embarrassment. "I'm educated in science and how to teach it. But obviously not in the ways of men."

But he did care about her, damn it. In ways he was only now beginning to realize. But that didn't mean he *loved* her. He wasn't ever going to open his heart up to that sort of pain again.

"Claudia—" he began remorsefully only to stop as she began to tug the opal from her finger. "What are you doing?"

She took his hand and placed the ring in the center of his palm. "Here," she said softly. "I think you should have this. After all, it once belonged to your grandfather. And there's no need for me to keep it anymore."

Before he could respond, she grabbed up her bag and left the cabin. Behind her, Hayden snatched up the bundle of love letters along with his grandfather's journal, then blew out the candle and hurried after her.

She was halfway down the wooden dock by the time he caught up to her and even then she seemed intent on getting to the car and starting their trip home.

No. Don't call it home, Hayden. A home is a place where a family lives. And you don't have one. You'll never have one.

"Claudia, I think we need to talk a little more about this."

She continued to walk in the direction of the car, her face forward, her eyes straight ahead. "Why? There's nothing left to be said."

Then why did he feel as though there was plenty left unsaid between them? Hayden wondered.

"Well, what are we going to do? Just leave things like this?"

By now they had reached the spot where Hayden had parked the Lincoln. At the passenger door Claudia turned and found his face in the semidarkness. He looked grim, almost angry and she couldn't figure why, except that she'd been an embarrassing pest to him these past few days.

"There are no *things* to do anything with, Hayden. You have your life to live and I have mine. As for the ring... Well, for some reason our grandparents wanted us to know what happened between them." She shrugged, while hoping he couldn't see the ache that was beginning to consume every part of her. "Now we've discovered the truth. It's finished. I'm relieved. You're relieved."

"Relieved hell!" he growled while snatching hold of her upper arm. "You just told me that you were in love with me! Now you act as though you'd simply been discussing the weather."

"I'm sure you would have found the weather more interesting." She purposely lifted her gaze to the sky. "Let's see if I can give you a current forecast. I'd say the temperature is around eighty and the humidity about the same. The barometric pressure is probably thirty and falling. The skies are clear except for the western horizon where there're a few stratocumulus clouds. In July, northern fronts are rarely ever weather-makers in south Texas, so I'd be safe to say the only chance of showers tomorrow would be the isolated kind that comes with the heating of the atmosphere. The dew point is a big factor here—"

The remainder of her weather forecast was suddenly blotted out as his lips captured hers in a totally devouring kiss that lifted her feet right off the ground.

She tried to remain stiff in his arms, to keep her mouth clamped against his sensual prodding, but after a few moments it was impossible. Everything inside her began to heat and melt. Everything inside her began to want him with a ferocity that stunned her.

Groaning, she flung her arms around his neck and clung to him as he kissed her lips over and over until they were both so breathless he was finally forced to drag his mouth away.

"Do you know how long I've wanted to do this? How much I've needed you like this?" he whispered roughly as he pressed kisses over her cheeks, along the side of her neck, and on downward to where the neckline of her peasant blouse exposed a faint bit of cleavage between her breasts. "Oh, Claudia, this is what's real. Not that stuff about the ring or the visions or destined love."

His lips were searing her skin with white-hot pleasure, making it physically impossible to push his head away. Tightening her hold on his neck, she fitted her hips to his. "I want you, too, Hayden. And maybe you're right," she murmured. "Maybe I don't need forever from you. This might be enough for as long as it lasts."

The invitation of her body sent a wave of heat roaring right through him, but her following words were like a douse of ice water, sobering him as nothing else could have. With slow, stiff movements, he eased himself away from her and wiped a hand over his face.

"Get in the car. Before I decide to take you up on your offer."

She made no move to do his bidding. Instead she tilted her chin defiantly up at him while the tip of her tongue came out to moisten her swollen lips. "Would that be so bad?" she asked.

He unlocked the door and practically pushed her inside.

"For someone like you? Yeah, real bad."

He closed the door with a resounding thud, then

loaded her bag into the back seat. Moments later he slid behind the steering wheel and tossed the bundled letters and journal onto the expanse of seat between them.

Her heart heavy, Claudia looked down at the worn, leather-bound journal, the yellowed, dog-eared envelopes. How could such beautiful, loving words seem like a mocking testimony now? she wondered sadly. This was not the way William and Betty Fay wanted things to be for their grandchildren. But then their intentions for a happy life together hadn't worked out, either.

"When we reach Victoria, you can leave me at a motel. I'll catch a flight back to Fort Worth from there," she said stiffly.

He cursed as he started the car and backed onto the street. "Forget it. The airport there doesn't support large airliners. You'd have to take a small commuter flight."

Finding it too painful to look at him, she stared out the passenger window as the shadowed docks began to slip from sight. She'd never sail on the *Stardust* again, she realized sorrowfully. Or see Hayden at the helm, his dark hair whipping in the breeze, his strong brown legs planted apart.

"I don't mind," she said, her voice rough with unshed tears. "I only left a few things at your house. You can send them to me later. Or better yet, give them to someone."

"Forget it," he repeated firmly. "I'm not leaving you at a motel anywhere! You're going back to my place whether you like it or not."

"I was only trying to spare you any more trouble."

His mocking laugh was like a twist of a knife in Claudia's heart.

"Too bad you didn't consider that before you ever came down here to south Texas."

"I wish I had, Hayden," she whispered thickly.

* * *

The next morning Hayden was cooking breakfast when Claudia entered the kitchen. She was wearing a beige sheath dress with a scooped-out neck and no sleeves. Her hair was pulled back into a tight French twist and golden hoops swung from her ears. In spite of her face being pale and lined with fatigue, she looked more beautiful to him than any woman he'd ever known. And he wondered how he was ever going to let her go.

"Good morning. I hope you're hungry," he told her. "I've cooked enough for two."

Before last night, when they'd squared off at each other, she would have smiled at him. Now her face remained sober, even stoic, and Hayden realized looking at her like this was like greeting a cloudy morning. He was grateful to see it, but it wasn't nearly as beautiful as bright sunshine.

"Yes. Thank you," she told him. "With a long day of traveling ahead of me, I should probably eat."

Telling himself he had no right to feel stung by her coolness, he turned his attention back to the frying ham in front of him. "The coffee has already dripped if you'd like a cup."

She went to the cabinet and took down a cup. From the corner of his eye, he watched her fill it, then add cream. When she carried it over to the breakfast bar and took a seat, he realized he was disappointed that she hadn't joined him at the cookstove.

Having her company these past few days had become a sweet treat for Hayden. And having her close had become an obsession, he supposed. No matter how hard he tried he couldn't seem to get enough of touching her, hearing her voice, seeing her smile.

But today that was all going to end. Unless a miracle happened. And Hayden didn't believe in miracles. Hell, he didn't even believe in himself anymore.

Once the breakfast food was cooked, he filled two plates and carried them over to the little dining table by the windows.

"This looks nice," she said as she eased into the seat across from his. "Thank you for being such a considerate host."

He didn't feel like a host and she didn't seem like a guest. For the short time she'd been here, she'd become a part of him and a part of this place. It was going to be hell getting her out of both, he realized.

"You're welcome, Claudia." He took a healthy swig of coffee, then doused his fried eggs with so much Tabasco sauce they turned orange. Hopefully, a little fire might pull him out of this lethargy that had come over him.

"I've already called the airport this morning," she wasted no time in telling him. "My flight leaves at nine-fifty this morning. Will we be back in San Antonio before then?"

Looking across the table, he caught her gaze, then wished he hadn't. The wounded shadows he saw there matched the dismal cloud spreading through his chest.

"I'll be ready to go as soon as we eat. You should have at least an hour to spare before your flight."

Nodding, she turned her attention to the food on her plate. Hayden sucked in a deep breath, then carefully released it.

"Claudia, you don't have to leave. You're welcome to stay here longer—if you'd like."

Her head jerked up and immediately her eyes filled

with unshed tears. "No thank you, Hayden. I'll be going back home today."

Home. She was going home. Why the hell did she keep calling it that? he asked himself. She lived in an apartment. Alone. That couldn't be any more of a home to her than this place was to him.

Her parents are in Fort Worth, he silently reminded himself. At least she had some sort of family. Yes, but she didn't have a man to share her life with. Someone to hold her and to make love to her. The way he wanted to.

"Why?"

She swallowed as a flood of emotions threatened to strangle her. "We both know why I can't stay here, Hayden."

He sighed with heavy resignation. "Yeah. I guess we do."

Claudia lowered her head over her plate while across from her, Hayden studied her glossy brown hair, her smooth honey-colored skin and the moist curve of her mouth. Damn it, he was crazy for letting his conscience get in the way. If Claudia was willing to have an affair with him, he should be happy to comply. Most any normal, red-blooded man would jump at the chance to have such a relationship with a woman like Claudia. So why wasn't he jumping? he mentally argued. Why wasn't he jerking her out of that chair and carrying her to the bedroom?

Because eventually she would want and need more from him than just a physical connection. When he couldn't give it, she'd leave. And Hayden was smart enough to know that losing her after having her would be far, far worse than telling her goodbye today.

"I've put your grandmother's letters in a holder for

you. They're in the living room on the coffee table. Don't forget to pick them up before we leave,'' he said quietly.

Clearing her throat, she looked up at him. ''Actually, I don't feel I have any right to the letters. They belonged to William and he was your grandfather.''

''Yes, but they were written by *your* grandmother. You should have them. I'll keep Granddad's journal. And the ring,'' he added. ''If that's what you want.''

Claudia nodded in agreement. ''It belongs here with you. I'll never wear it again. I couldn't bear to see your grandfather now.''

Her voice broke to a strangled whisper on the last words and the sound tore a hole right through Hayden.

''Claudia—'' He reached for her hand, but she avoided his touch by quickly rising to her feet.

''I'd better go pack the last of my things.''

''Your breakfast—''

''I'm finished,'' she blurted, then hurried out of the room.

Once she'd disappeared out the door, Hayden tossed down his fork and stared blindly at the birds feeding beyond the windows.

She was finished all right, he thought dully. With breakfast and with him. Their time together was over. Now all he had to do was stand back and watch her walk out of his life.

Chapter Ten

A week later Claudia entered her parents' house and found her mother in the kitchen preparing shrimp salad for their evening meal.

"Hi, Mom."

The moment Marsha heard her daughter's voice she turned away from the cabinet counter and greeted Claudia with a bright smile.

"Oh, honey, I'm so glad you could come over this evening. With your dad gone on that fishing trip down in the hill country, this place is entirely too quiet for me."

Joining her mother at the row of oak cabinets, Claudia picked up a stick of celery and munched at one end. "You should get out more, Mom. Maybe take a part-time job."

Marsha laughed at her daughter's suggestion. "I'm not that bored," she said as she dropped the last few pieces of lettuce she'd been tearing into a large bowl. Once the task was finished, she stepped back to inspect her daughter with a keen eye. "You look so thin, darling. Haven't you been eating?"

Claudia shrugged. "It's summer, Mom. With the temperatures hanging around a hundred, I don't have much of an appetite."

"Hmm, that never seemed to bother you before."

A grimace tightened her gaunt features. "Well, there has been a lot of things going on in my life," she reasoned. "Learning my grandmother was madly in love with a man other than my grandfather is rather jolting."

Sighing, Marsha turned back to the salad she was making. "Yes, what you discovered down in south Texas has shocked all of us. Not to say we disapprove of Betty Fay's behavior," she added with a shake of her head. "I mean, what is there to disapprove about? She met and fell in love with this William Bedford long before she met and married Amos Westfield. And from the way her letters read, once they parted, they never saw each other again, so it wasn't like they cheated on anybody."

"Not physically, at least," Claudia replied.

With a look of bewilderment Marsha asked, "What other kind of cheating is there?"

Rolling her eyes with disbelief, Claudia opened the cabinet and began to pull down plates and glasses. "Mom, think about it. Emotionally. Spiritually. How would you feel if you discovered Daddy had loved and longed for another woman all the time he'd been married to you? Wouldn't that wound you?"

Sudden understanding lit Marsha's face. "I hadn't thought about it like that. You're right, honey. That would be awful. Even worse than what Tony did to you," she said, then realizing how that must have sounded, she touched a hand to her daughter's shoulder.

"I'm sorry, Claudia. I shouldn't have said that. My mouth has always worked faster than my brain."

Claudia carried the plates and glasses over to a small glass-topped table situated at one end of the kitchen. Her mother was right, she thought. Tony's philandering had hurt. But Hayden's rejection of her love had virtually crushed her. This past week she'd been trying to forget him, trying to tell herself that she was better off without him in her life. But so far she hadn't convinced her heart.

"Don't apologize, Mom. Talking about Tony doesn't bother me anymore."

She placed the plates and glasses on straw place mats, then walked back to the cabinet. As she dug silverware from a drawer, Marsha glanced at her.

"I think you really mean that."

"I do mean it. That part of my past is over and done with. I'm very relieved I didn't make the mistake of marrying him."

Marsha smiled, although her eyes were filled with concern. "I'm glad to hear it. But if that's the case, then why aren't you happy? You've solved the cause of your visions. You haven't been having any more of them, have you?"

Claudia shook her head. "No. And I don't ever expect to. Now that I've gotten rid of the ring."

"Ah, the ring," she said perceptively. "You know, your dad and I were both surprised that you left the opal with Hayden Bedford. Being a gift from your grandmother, it had always meant so much to you."

Claudia clutched the silverware in her fist and stared at a spot on the wall. "Well, the ring just doesn't mean the same now. I'd always considered it a symbol of love. But it didn't turn out that way."

Leaning her hip against the cabinet counter, Marsha

folded her arms across her breasts and leveled a pointed look at her daughter. "I can't imagine you saying such a thing. Now that we know about the love story between Betty Fay and William and how he'd given her the ring with a promise to marry her—well, you couldn't get a more perfect symbol of lasting love. Haven't you thought about it in those terms?"

Claudia carried the silverware to the table and arranged it on the place mats. "Of course I have," she told her mother. In fact, she'd thought of little else. That's why it hurt even more to think of the ring and Hayden. But she couldn't explain this to her mother without admitting that she'd fallen in love with the man and he'd rejected her. "But the ring has caused me a lot of misery that I'd like to forget."

Pondering her daughter's remarks, Marsha ignored the partially prepared salad.

"Actually, your dad was relieved you left the ring behind. He was concerned you might let your thinking about the ring sway you in the wrong direction." Marsha waved her hand in a dismissive way. "But I told him that was silly. You were too levelheaded to let yourself fall for a total stranger. You're just not that kind of young woman."

No, Claudia thought sadly, she was the dull, scientific kind. No one would dream that she might long for a man to take her into his arms and make passionate love to her. No one understood that her teaching career was only a part of what she wanted out of life. Not even her parents realized how much she longed for a husband and family of her own. Yet now that she'd fallen in love with Hayden, she couldn't envision herself with either. Unlike Betty Fay, she couldn't go on with her life and marry someone else.

"Uh, Mom, is that salad finished? I'm getting hungry."

Marsha quickly turned back to the bowl of raw vegetables. "Sorry, honey. It will only be a few minutes. In the meantime, would you make a pitcher of iced tea? And you need to set another place at the table."

Surprised by this news, Claudia looked at her. "Why? Is someone else going to be eating supper with us?"

Before Marsha could reply, a female voice sounded at the open doorway leading into the kitchen.

"Knock. Knock."

Claudia turned to see Liz entering the room. A dish covered with aluminum foil was in her hands and a wide smile was on her impish face. Just the sight of her dear friend brought a sting of tears to the back of Claudia's eyes.

"Liz!" She rushed forward and hugged the other woman. "What are you doing here?"

"Your mother invited me. She thought you needed a bit of cheering and you know me, I'm usually good for a laugh, if nothing else."

"Oh, I'm so glad you came," Claudia exclaimed then glanced affectionately at her mother. "You kept this a secret."

Marsha laughed. "I know it probably amazes you, but sometimes your mother can keep her mouth shut."

For the next hour the three women relaxed over the simple meal and once it was over Marsha shooed the two younger women out the back door with a plate loaded with chocolate brownies. Beneath the deep shade of a willow tree, the two women took seats in cushioned lawn chairs. Claudia handed the plate of brownies to her friend, then quickly declined when Liz offered it back to her.

Leaning over in her chair, Liz placed the plate of remaining brownies on a nearby table, then turned back to Claudia.

"Okay, now that your mother can't hear us I can tell you that you look like hell! And why the heck haven't you called me? From what she told me on the phone, you've been back in Fort Worth for a week or more! I thought we were friends! Good friends!"

Claudia sighed. "We are, Liz. I just haven't been up to talking to anyone. In fact, this evening is the first time I've been away from the apartment since I got back."

Still not mollified, Liz tossed her red head, then leveled a pointed look at Claudia. "It doesn't take a whole lot of energy to punch a few numbers," she said accusingly. "You just didn't want to tell me what went on down there."

Wearily, Claudia pinched the bridge of her nose. "I'm sure Mom called you and filled you in on what happened."

"She told me about William Bedford and your grandmother and how you found the letters and journals. She also told me you left the opal with Hayden."

"That's true," Claudia said stiffly. "The ring is now his."

Groaning, Liz leaned over and plucked another brownie from the plate. "Your grandmother must be spinning in her grave right about now."

Claudia scowled at her friend. "I doubt that. I think she's probably happy that her lover's grandson now possesses the ring."

"She wanted *you* to have the ring. She promised it would lead you to true love!"

With a bitter snort, Claudia gazed out across the neatly clipped lawn. Her heart was splitting right down the middle and there was nothing she could do to ease the pain. If true love felt like this, she wished she'd never found it.

"That was just a bunch of Gran's sentimental malarkey. I don't believe in it any more than you do."

Liz shook her head. "Don't classify me as a nonbeliever. I chase after rainbows, remember. And if I recall correctly, you didn't believe in visions, either—until you had one." Intent on making her point, she squared around in her chair so that she was facing Claudia head-on. "How can you say for sure that the ring wouldn't eventually lead you to your soul mate? It took you all the way to south Texas. It helped you discover the truth about your grandmother's young life. Now you've given it away and—" Liz's words came to an abrupt halt and her eyes grew wide. "Wait just a darn minute here. Maybe it did lead you to your soul mate. Maybe that's why you look sick. You're in love with Hayden Bedford!"

Claudia opened her mouth to give Liz a quick, loud denial, but she was unable to get so much as a sound past her lips.

Seeing her hunch was correct, Liz swallowed the last of her brownie, then brushed the crumbs from her fingers before she urged, "Tell me about him."

Dropping her head, Claudia mumbled, "There's nothing to tell, Liz. Except that I've made a fool of myself. Again."

Suddenly contrite, Liz reached over and touched Claudia's shoulder. "It couldn't be that bad."

Closing her eyes, Claudia shook her head. "I've never been so miserable in my life, Liz. I wish… I should have never worn that ring again. Especially after I discovered it was causing those visions."

Gravely, Liz studied Claudia's lowered head. "I guess I'm the cause of that," she said glumly. "I dared you to hunt for the man in those visions. I suppose I was hoping you'd meet him and instantly fall in love."

It might not have been instant, Claudia thought, but she'd fallen. Only she'd fallen for the wrong man. A man that would never return her love.

Her voice hollow, she said, "That would have been impossible. The man in my visions is dead."

Liz shivered outwardly. "How eerie to think all that time you were seeing a ghost."

Claudia lifted her head. "I wasn't seeing a ghost," she said with a frown. "William was…well, he was just the image of a man who came to me to tell me something. And eventually he did."

"Funny that you should picture him back in his young life when he was in love with your grandmother."

"He was *always* in love with my grandmother," Claudia corrected her as she pushed fingers through her brown hair, then rubbed at the dull ache in her temples. "Although you are right about the fact that I envisioned him as he was during the time their affair was ongoing."

"What about Hayden?" Liz wanted to know. "I guess your whole story about the ring came as a shock to him."

Claudia laughed bitterly. "He thought I was trying to pull some sort of con. At the very least, he thought I was a nut case. I'm still not sure why he didn't just let me leave San Antonio that first day we met. I would have been a lot better off if he had."

"Really?"

Liz's simple question caused Claudia's brow to wrinkle with confusion. "Why yes. I wouldn't be going through all this pain."

The grimace on Liz's face said she was clearly disappointed in Claudia's reasoning. "Maybe not. But you wouldn't have any answers, either. And you would have missed falling in love."

Claudia's features tightened. "I wish I had missed it!" she muttered, then with a tormented groan, she shook her head. "No. That's not true. The idea of not ever knowing Hayden would be like never seeing a rainbow in the sky."

The agony lacing Claudia's voice had Liz quickly reaching for her hand. Giving it a comforting squeeze, she said, "You must love him a lot."

Nodding, Claudia whispered, "I'll never love anyone else, Liz. My grandmother was right. The ring did lead me to my true love. She just didn't know that Hayden wouldn't love me back."

"Oh, Claudia. What happened?"

Shrugging with defeat, Claudia focused on the flowering shrubs growing alongside the privacy fence that surrounded the yard. "Nothing really. I fell in love and he didn't. It's that simple."

"Nothing about a man and woman's relationship could be that simple," Liz argued. "There has to be more. Is he married or something?"

"He's divorced. His wife was unfaithful and I think he blames himself for that. Since her betrayal and the breakup of his marriage... Well, he doesn't want a woman in his life. And before you ask, yes, he made that clear to me right from the start. My heart just didn't listen."

Liz grimaced. "A woman's heart rarely listens to logic. Besides, it's pretty obvious to me that the two of you were meant to be together. Or William and Betty Fay went to a lot of trouble for nothing."

Sadly, Claudia looked over at her friend. "That's what I thought. But Hayden doesn't believe in love anymore. He lost both his parents in a short time span. And then his marriage ended and his wife was gone. As far as he's concerned, nothing lasts."

Thoughtful now, Liz reached for another brownie. "The man is scared, Claudia. He's afraid to love you, because he's afraid of losing you. And who could blame him? He probably feels like he isn't supposed to have a family."

"I know *that*, Liz. But knowing it doesn't help me get over the man! It doesn't help this ache inside me."

Liz bit off a huge hunk of brownie and chewed. "Get over the man! What are you talking about? You're not supposed to get over him. You've got to go back down there and make him see reason!"

Claudia jerked upright and scooted to the edge of the lawn chair. "Oh, no! No way am I going back to San Antonio. Not to see Hayden. Walking away from him at the airport was the hardest thing I've ever done in my life. I won't put myself through that sort of agony again."

"You're in misery now. What would be the difference?" Liz wanted to know.

"At least here he can't humiliate me."

"He can't love you, either."

Groaning with frustration, Claudia rose to her feet and began to pace back and forth. "I've been back in Fort Worth for over a week now. I haven't heard a word from him. And I'm quite certain I won't."

"Then you'd better decide right now whether this man means enough to you to make you swallow your pride and head south again."

Claudia stared at her friend. "Liz, it isn't a matter of

pride! I'm not a femme fatale, like you. I'm a practical science teacher. I don't know the first thing about how to make a man fall for me!''

Leaving her seat, Liz walked over to where Claudia stood and laid a reassuring hand on her shoulder. ''You're out of your mind if you think I'm a femme fatale, Claudia. When it comes to love and men, I'm just as scared and lost as you are.''

Surprised by Liz's comment, she studied her friend's face. ''But you've been married, Liz. You're beautiful and confident. Men are always asking you for dates.''

She smiled ruefully. ''I can fake being beautiful and confident. But in truth, my marriage ended, so that goes to show you how much of a femme fatale I am. And just because I'm asked out on dates doesn't mean I'm going to find love—the right love.'' She squeezed Claudia's shoulder. ''Believe me, Claudia, it's a precious commodity. Some people search for a lifetime and never find it. That's why...well, what I'm trying to say is if you really love this guy, then you ought to at least give it one more try.''

Could she? Claudia wondered. Leaving Hayden once had been bad enough. If she had to do it a second time, it might kill every hope, every longing, she'd ever had for a husband and family.

''I'll think about it, Liz,'' she finally promised.

Smiling, Liz gave her shoulder a little shake. ''Don't think about it too long. You need to strike while the iron is hot.''

At the same time on a dusty rig site two hundred miles west of San Antonio, Hayden lifted the ringing cell phone from the dashboard of his pickup.

''Hayden, here.''

"It's Lottie, Mr. Bedford. I was just checking to see if Vince had gotten there yet with the crew."

"Not yet. The last I heard he was about thirty minutes away." Normally, Hayden didn't make firsthand visits to rig sites that his crews were excavating and building for a drilling company. Most always he left that up to Vince, his right-hand man. But this particular site was going to be built on difficult terrain and the job was going to be costly, not to mention problematic. Hayden wanted to be here to get everything tapped off right from the very beginning.

"Good," she said, then quickly asked, "What are you doing?"

Hayden rolled his eyes. Lottie was irreplaceable, but sometimes she could be too much like a mother. "I'm sitting here in this damn truck burning up, that's what! And by the way, what are you doing on the phone? It's nearly seven-thirty, you're not supposed to be at the office at this late hour."

"I'm not at the office. I'm at home. And I called because I happened to be worried about you. This morning when you left, you just weren't yourself."

Hayden hadn't been himself for days. Not since he'd left Claudia at the airport. It surprised him that Lottie was just now noticing. Maybe he'd been doing a better job of hiding his feelings than he'd thought.

"There's nothing wrong, other than the fact that I need about five more new hands. Good ones that I can trust."

"I put several résumés on your desk this afternoon. Maybe some of them will be fruitful."

He drummed his fingers against the steering wheel and peered toward the red-gold haze of sunlight dropping rapidly toward the western horizon. If he was lucky, he'd get home before two in the morning. "I'll go over them tomorrow."

Lottie let out a gasp of surprise. "You're not staying out there tonight?"

"There's no place to stay, Lottie. Unless I drive up to San Angelo, and that's out of the way. Besides, I have things back at the office I need to get to first thing in the morning."

"Don't you think you'll be needing a little sleep? It's not like you're going to be able to drive back home in an hour."

"More like three or four," Hayden said as he wiped sweat from his forehead with the back of his sleeve, then wearily pinched the bridge of his nose.

The few days he'd spent with Claudia had shown him a different side of life. Work, money, the company was not his sole purpose for living. At least, it shouldn't be. Yet somehow he'd let Bedford Roustabout take him over. Especially after his parents had died and Saundra had moved out. Once his family was gone, he'd not had anything to fill his life, except Bedford Roustabout. Now a part of him wished he'd listened to Lottie years ago and hired someone to help him carry his late father's workload, rather than try to do it all himself.

"I always thought you were trying to kill yourself," she said in a disgruntled voice. "Now I'm sure of it. When are you going to open your eyes and realize you can't run this company by yourself?"

Wondering if the older woman could see inside his head, he said wearily, "I don't know, Lottie. And I'm not in any mood to discuss it now."

"You're never in any mood for anything," she snapped at him. "I'm just wondering how long it's going to take before you'll admit what's wrong with you!"

He pulled the phone from his ear and stared at it. Lottie had never been afraid to mince words with him. She was like family and she knew it. Still, she'd never spoken to him in quite this tone before.

"Is there something wrong with me?" he asked blandly.

She cursed in his ear. "Ms. Westfield is your problem! Furthermore, you know it. What I'd like to know is when you're going to do something about it?"

He closed his eyes as Claudia's image washed through him. It hurt to think of her, yet her memory never left him for more than a few moments at a time. "After what Saundra put me through, you can ask that? Damn it, Lottie, what do you think I am, one of those people who thrive on pain?"

To his amazement, she cursed again and this time the word she used turned his ears red. "Just because you got yourself tangled up with the wrong woman once, doesn't mean you have to live the rest of your life as a monk."

"For your information I haven't been living as a monk," he practically snarled.

Lottie snorted. "You can't lie to me any better than you could lie to your own mother. I haven't worn blinders for the past three years, Mr. Bedford. You've been going around with ice water in your veins. Marilyn Monroe could have walked into your office and you wouldn't have so much as perked an ear in her direction. But Ms. Westfield comes in and—"

"Forget about Claudia," he interrupted. "She's gone back home and there's nothing I can do about it! But there is something I can do about you if you don't quit sticking your nose in my personal life. And that's fire you!"

Lottie dismissed his threat with a loud laugh. "What personal life? You don't have any."

The quick retort that came to Hayden's tongue stayed there as he heard the click of the receiver on the other end of the line.

Damn it, she'd hung up on him. His own secretary! He wasn't going to let her get by with such disrespect. And he sure as hell wasn't going to let her accuse him of being a half-dead man with ice water in his veins!

Quickly, before his ire cooled, he punched in Lottie's home telephone number. The moment she answered, he barked, "Lottie! What are you trying to do to me?"

The older woman sighed. "Believe it or not, Mr. Bedford, I'm trying to help you. And I think it's time I let you in on something."

Lottie's tone of voice put Hayden on instant alert. "What are you talking about?"

There was a short pause, then Lottie said, "Shortly after I went to work for your grandfather he approached me with a task that he called...well, personal. I was to gather information on a woman named Betty Fay Westfield. And down through the years that's what I did. I have a file on the woman and her family locked in a drawer in my office."

After all the astounding things he'd discovered the past two weeks, Lottie's confession shouldn't have surprised him. But in truth, he was bowled over. Learning that William had discreetly kept up with Betty Fay's well-being reinforced the fact that his love for the woman had been true and everlasting. "You mean, you knew who Claudia was that day she came to the office?"

"Yes. That's why I almost didn't give her an appointment. I was afraid she might dredge up things better left in the past. But then I realized that denying her an appointment wouldn't be enough to stop her from seeing you. And now I'm glad I didn't. I think all of this has happened because the two of you were meant to be together."

For long moments Hayden remained silent as he tried to absorb everything Lottie had just told him, then he groaned. "Not you, too, Lottie."

"Mr. Bedford—"

"Save it, Lottie. Vince is driving up. I'll talk to you later about that file."

Spared from dealing with Lottie any longer, he clicked off the phone, then slapped a hard hat on his head. He'd been wrong a few minutes ago, he thought as he walked over to where Vince had parked. Work was what he needed. And lots of it. Otherwise, he just might see how empty his life was without Claudia.

Seven hours later Hayden let himself into the house. After a quick shower, he switched on a lamp at the head of the bed, then turned down the covers and sat on the edge of the mattress.

He was bone-tired, yet his weariness could not be fixed by several hours of deep sleep. Since Claudia had left, he'd been living in mental torment and he was beginning to wonder how much longer he could hold up under the strain.

Lottie had been right about one thing. He'd been living like a monk, burying himself in his work and trying to forget he was a man alone. Until Claudia had waltzed into his office, he thought grimly. For some reason he couldn't understand, her soft gentle looks and prim attitude had woken him from his half-dead existence. Now he couldn't get her out of his mind. Or his heart.

Groaning at that last thought, he desperately raked fingers through his damp hair. As he did, his eyes settled on his grandfather's journal lying on the bedside table. Beside it, the opal winked beneath the artificial glow of the lamp.

Had Claudia missed the ring? he wondered. Or was she glad to finally be rid of it? Of him?

Afraid of those questions, he picked up the ring and stared down at the simple stone. It still seemed incredible to him that a little piece of jewelry had caused such a traumatic change to his life. Because of the ring, Claudia had entered his life and for a few short days he'd been tempted to let himself believe again, to hope for love and the family he'd always wanted. Tempted, but not persuaded. So he'd sent her away in hopes of saving her and himself a major heartache.

What do you think you're going through now, Hayden? What else do you need to convince you that what you feel for Claudia and what she feels for you is real— the kind of love that will never die? A lightning bolt out of the blue? A vision of your own? Would that be enough to open your eyes and your heart?

Mentally cursing at the nagging little voice in his ear, he clutched the ring tightly in his fist and stared at the journal. His grandfather had given the opal to the woman he'd first loved, then lost. And from what he'd read in the journal, Betty Fay had given William a wristwatch somewhere around the same time he'd given her the ring. Where was the watch now? Hayden wondered. Somewhere out there causing someone else to be plagued with unexplained visions? Or had it been tossed away, discarded like a broken dream?

Sighing because no answers came to him, Hayden leaned over to return the ring to the nightstand and switch off the light. But before he could finish either task, an image suddenly came to him from out of nowhere. And the picture was so clear and unexpected that he was momentarily stunned motionless.

He knew where his grandfather's watch was hidden. It was in this very house!

Bolting off the bed, Hayden hurried down the hallway to the small room he used as an office. On a shelf with his grandfather's picture and several other souvenirs was the model of a sailboat he'd put together as a small boy. Even though it didn't exactly resemble the *Stardust*, Hayden had painted the name in tiny letters on the side of the boat and presented it to his grandfather as a birthday gift. Years later, after Hayden had grown up, William had given the boat back to him and told him to always keep it, even after he was dead and gone.

At the time Hayden had considered William's bequest rather overly sentimental. After all, it was just a toy. But it did signify the love of sailing they shared together, so Hayden had hung on to the miniature *Stardust*. Now he thought he understood why William had been so nostalgic about the boat.

Picking up a penknife from his desk, Hayden carefully eased the hull away from the deck until the wooden model was separated into two pieces.

"Well, I'll be damned," he murmured.

Nestled in the hollow section of the boat's hull, the watch was carefully wrapped in layers of cotton. Hayden's hands were actually shaking by the time he'd folded it all back and exposed the silver-plated timepiece.

On the back of the face, the simple words were inscribed. *To my darling, Bill. Eternally, Betty Fay 1943*.

Feeling as if someone had whacked him in the knees,

Hayden sank into the leather desk chair and stared up at his grandfather's photograph.

"You wanted me to find this, didn't you?" he whispered with sudden understanding. "You're trying to tell me that Claudia is my one true love. Just like Betty Fay was yours."

The photograph didn't answer. But then it didn't have to. For the first time in years, Hayden was listening with his heart.

Chapter Eleven

Claudia placed a pair of jean shorts into the leather duffel bag with the clothes she'd already packed, then glanced at the telephone. One call to the airport and she'd be on her way back to San Antonio. Back to Hayden.

Since her talk with Liz last night, she'd been telling herself that her friend was right. Even though her relationship with Hayden was definitely one-sided, she had to convince him the world wouldn't fall apart if he gave the two of them a chance to be together. But telling herself and actually taking a step to do such a thing were two entirely different things.

Each time she'd tried to pick up the telephone and call the airport, she got the feeling it was a coiled snake ready to bite.

The telephone can't bite, but Hayden can and will.

Groaning at the heckling voice inside her head, she sank onto the edge of the bed and dropped her head into her hands.

What did she think she was doing? she asked herself. Just because she was miserable being apart from Hayden didn't mean his heart was in the same sorry state of affairs. Now that he had her out of his hair and the mystery of the ring solved, he'd probably had a wonderful week. More than likely he'd been whistling a happy tune every morning at the breakfast table.

Squeezing her eyes shut, she tried not to picture the two of them eating at the little table together while outside the windows the mourning doves cooed and flirted with their mates. She tried to push the sight of Hayden's tanned face and hard body lying against the Matagorda sand and to forget the urgent, needy kisses he'd pressed on her lips and face. But everything about him was branded into her mind and heart, making it impossible to forget.

She had no choice, she thought. Hayden meant too much to her to simply give up and let his jaded attitude ruin their chance at a happy life together. Somehow she had to convince him that the ring had brought them together for a reason, and that was to spend the rest of their lives together.

Quickly, before her burst of courage could wane, Claudia jumped to her feet and snatched up the phone. The airport number was scribbled on a notepad resting on the edge of the desk. Breathing deeply, she began to rapidly punch the digits.

She was about to push the last button when the doorbell shrilled loudly. The unexpected sound caused her to jump and drop the receiver. By the time she'd picked it up and planted it back to her ear, a recorded voice was telling her the call could not be connected.

"Damn it," she muttered to herself. "Someone has rotten timing."

Just as she hurried out of the bedroom, the doorbell rang again, this time with impatient persistence.

"I'm coming. Just a minute," she called as she entered the tiny foyer that separated the entrance of her apartment from the living room.

Even though it was broad daylight, she cautiously glanced through the peephole. Since the caller was not standing within her view, she called, "Who is it?"

She heard a shuffle of feet, then a familiar male voice. "It's Hayden, Claudia."

Hayden! What was he doing in Fort Worth? Stunned, her hands shaking, she quickly unlatched the door and swung it open. The sight of him standing on the other side of the threshold caused her to take a quick, deep breath.

"Hello, Claudia."

She swallowed and touched a hand to her mussed hair and bare face. He was wearing a crisp blue-and-white pin-striped shirt, dark blue jeans and black Western boots made of expensive ostrich skin. Yet even if he'd been wearing oily coveralls, he would have looked like heaven to her. "Hayden, what are you doing here?"

Inclining his head toward the small space behind her, he said, "If you don't mind me coming in I'd rather explain inside."

Too flustered for words, she motioned for him to enter and as he stepped past her, her knees grew frighteningly weak. Just following him into the living room without collapsing was a major feat.

"I was—"

"I know—"

Their tangled voices caused their gazes to meet. Claudia's already-pounding heart began to beat even harder and she placed a hand on the back of an armchair to brace her wobbly knees.

"I realize I should have called and warned you that I was coming. But I didn't want to give you the opportunity to get prepared," he said.

Bewildered, she stared at him. "I don't understand, Hayden. Prepared for what?"

His expression sheepish, he shrugged. "To throw me out."

It was all she could do to keep her mouth from dropping open. "Why would I want to do something like that?"

Her innocent question caused his lips to twist with self-mockery. He should have realized Claudia couldn't be grudgeful. Nor was there a guileful bone in her body. But then he should have realized a lot of things before he'd let her walk away from him back in San Antonio.

Stepping toward her, he said in a low, shameful voice, "Because I hurt you."

Her brown eyes continued to desperately search his face for explanations. "Yes, you did. But I don't think you really wanted to hurt me. Besides, the whole thing that happened between us was...well, it was mostly my fault." She stopped long enough to moisten her lips with the tip of her tongue. "It was foolish of me to expect you to want the same things I did. Especially since we've only known each other a very short time."

His expression grave, he closed the last step between them and placed his hands on her shoulders. "What things are you talking about, Claudia? Tell me," he softly invited.

Doubts and fears swirled inside her. Just because he'd shown up here at her apartment didn't mean he'd changed his mind about the two of them being together, she told herself. Still, the way he was looking at her made every particle of her being want to fall into his arms and never let go.

Lifting her chin, she said, "I think you know how I feel about you, Hayden. If you came all the way up here to Fort Worth to hear me say that's changed, then you're going to be disappointed. I love you whether you like it or not."

The relief he felt was so great, he actually groaned out loud. Then before she could guess his intentions, he pulled her into his arms and cradled her head against his shoulder. "Oh, Claudia! All during my drive up here I was so afraid. I'd behaved like such a jackass I wasn't sure you'd be willing to see me again, much less still care about me."

Totally bewildered now, she eased her head back far enough from his shoulder to enable her to view the profile of his face. "Hayden, I still don't understand why you're here. What—"

"I'm here for three reasons," he quickly interrupted.

Cradling her face in his palms, he looked into her eyes. "First of all, I want to apologize."

Just being this near him, having him touch her was enough to send her head spinning. "Apologize for what? Not loving me?"

His head swung back and forth with regret. "No. For not being brave enough to admit it while you were still in San Antonio with me."

She couldn't believe what she was hearing and the shock must have shown on her face because he smiled ruefully and said, "I know you're probably going to tell me that my declaration of love is a little late in coming. But I guess I was just too damned afraid, Claudia. Everything about the ring and the visions seemed so far-fetched and then when we discovered the letters and the journal I didn't know what to think. About our grandparents. About you and me. And most of all about the things in life that we can't necessarily see.''

"Like love," she said softly.

His blue eyes turned tender as his palm stroked the top of her soft, brown hair. "Yes, like love. Deep down I knew it existed. I'd loved my parents very much. And for what it was worth, I'd loved Saundra. But I'd lost all of them and after that— Well, I guess a part of me died and my faith in human emotions died along with me.''

Her heart aching with love and hope, she slipped her arms around his waist. "So what made you change your mind?''

"That's the second reason I'm here," he said, dropping his hand from her face long enough to fish the watch out of his jeans' pocket. "I want to show you something.''

Intrigued now, Claudia looked at the silver watch in his palm. Her brow wrinkled as a snippet from one of Betty Fay's letters raced through her mind. "That watch belonged to your grandfather. My grandmother gave it to him! And after all these years you found it!''

He nodded. "Last night I was holding the ring, thinking about you and how miserable I was without you and then the watch entered my mind. I was hoping if the ring had somehow managed to survive, then maybe the watch was still around somewhere. I was trying to tell myself it had probably been thrown away when all of a sudden something told me exactly where to look for it. Pretty incredible, huh?'' He motioned for her to take the watch. "Read the back," he urged.

Claudia did as he suggested and by the time she lifted

her eyes back up to his, they were filled with tears. "Oh, Hayden. William and Betty Fay loved each other so much, yet they never got the chance to share their lives. We can't let that happen to us."

She handed the watch back to him. He slipped it onto his wrist, then cradled his hand against the side of her face. "I have no intentions of letting that happen, Claudia. That's the third reason I'm here."

Her brows lifted. "The third?"

His smile tender, he used the pads of his thumbs to wipe away the tears that had fallen onto her cheeks. "Yeah. The third reason I'm here is the most important one of all. And that's to ask you to marry me."

Claudia supposed his proposal should have shocked her, too. But it didn't. There was too much love in his blue eyes, too much need in the hands touching her, for him to want to settle for anything less than marriage between them.

"You said after Saundra you never wanted to marry again."

Sliding his hands down her back, he gathered her close against him. "What Saundra and I had between us was never a real marriage. I can see that now. The only thing we really shared was the same bedroom and it takes much more than that for love to endure."

Snuggling even closer, Claudia tilted her face up to his. "Yes, our grandparents are a good example of that. I'm certain their love lives on still and I'm even more certain their love brought us together."

Bending his head, he pressed his cheek against hers. "A few days ago, I would have called you crazy."

His remark put a teasing curve to her lips. "You did, Hayden."

He chuckled. "I guess I did, didn't I?"

"You've been a hard man to convince."

Groaning, he shook his head with regret. "I have to confess, Claudia, even after your visions led us to the *Stardust* and the hidden letters and journal, I still didn't want to believe what I was seeing. To think that some invisible force was leading us…well, it went against all my common sense. And then when I started falling in love with you I guess I really went into denial about what was happening."

Her brown eyes filled with understanding. "Believe me, Hayden, I felt the same way at first. A science teacher deals with proven facts. I didn't want to think that something so unexplainable could be happening to me. But then I met you and everything inside me began to change. Especially after you kissed me," she added impishly.

His forefinger lifted to her soft lips and then his head bent toward hers. "And I think it's way past time for me to do it again, don't you?" he murmured.

As his lips settled over hers, golden rays of happiness glowed in her heart and she kissed him back with unabashed passion and all the love that went with it.

"Whew! I think we'd better head down to the courthouse and purchase a marriage license today. Texas has a two-day waiting period. Damn it!"

Her eyes widened and she laughed with wonder. "You mean we're going to get married that soon?"

Hayden tightened his hold on her. "That's why I drove up here instead of taking a flight. So we could load all your things in my truck and take them back to San Antonio with us." His expression suddenly serious, he traced his fingertips against her cheek. "Claudia, tell me if I'm asking too much of you. I realize how much your teaching career means to you. I know it's important for you to work with children and you have your job here—''

"Hayden," she gently interrupted, "I'd bet my bottom dollar that there's plenty of schools in San Antonio that could use a science teacher. And as for children—'' She paused as her cheeks tinged pink and a soft smile tilted her lips. "I'm hoping we'll eventually have a few of our own for me to take care of."

Overwhelmed with emotion, Hayden buried his face in the curve of her neck. "Oh, Claudia, I thought it was meant for me to never have a family. Thank God you came along with that ring of yours and turned my thinking upside down."

"Hmm. And to think I wanted to throw it away," she said with a soft laugh.

Easing away from her, he dug once again into the front pocket of his jeans. Holding up the opal, he said, "Speaking of rings, I haven't had a chance to get you an engagement ring yet. Will this one do for right now?"

The sight of the ring and all it stood for caused a wave of emotion to tighten her throat and to turn her voice husky. "I can't imagine a more perfect one."

Gently he lifted her left hand and slipped it onto her finger. "Do you think it will cause you to start seeing my grandfather's face again?"

Shaking her head, she raised up on tiptoe to press a kiss to his cheek. "I somehow believe that William and Betty Fay know they've accomplished what they set out to do. And that was to bring us together. Now they're going to leave it up to us to finish the rest of the job."

The look he slanted her was both amused and curious. "'Job'?"

She tilted her face up to his. "Yes, my darling. To love each other for the rest of our lives."

"Hmm. That won't be a job," he whispered against her lips. "It'll be a pleasure."

Epilogue

The late evening shadows of the spreading oaks made a cool canopy over Claudia and Hayden as they strolled hand in hand behind the house that had been their home since their marriage nearly fifty years ago.

Across the groomed yard, family and friends filled the screened-in back porch and spilled over to the shaded patio. Laughter and bursts of animated conversations punctuated the warm summer air.

"I think Gayla has enjoyed her birthday party, don't you?" Hayden asked his wife. "She seemed totally surprised when she walked in and saw all the decorations and guests and gifts."

Claudia laughed softly. "Our granddaughter thought she was coming over here to give the dogs a bath. It's a good thing her mother and I had thought to have something a little nicer than a pair of jeans and T-shirt to change into. Otherwise she might not have ever forgiven us. Especially when there's several male friends of hers here tonight."

Hayden slipped his arm around the back of his wife's waist. "Speaking of male friends, when are you going to give Gayla the ring?"

Claudia glanced over her shoulder to the group of young people gathered around the barbecue grill. "I've told her mother to send her out here to us so we'd have more privacy. Hopefully she'll be along in a few minutes."

"I don't think our son much likes the idea of his daughter getting the opal. He's not ready to lose her to a husband yet," Hayden said with a bit of fond amusement. "But I told Will to look at his parents' long and happy marriage and that ought to be enough to make him feel good about Gayla wearing the opal."

Smiling with a love that had only grown deeper with time, Claudia lifted her face up to her husband's. Although time had lined his face and grayed his once dark hair, he was still as handsome to her as the day they'd repeated their marriage vows. "The years have passed by so swiftly, my darling. It seems like only yesterday that I walked into your office and saw you for the very first time. I was shocked."

He chuckled at the memory. "I was shocked, too. Especially when I kissed you. I thought a firecracker had gone off in my hands." Halting their slow walk, he pulled her into his arms. "And you still do that to me, honey. You know that, don't you?"

To make sure she got the message, he bent his head and placed a lengthy kiss on her lips.

Behind them, a young woman discreetly cleared her throat. "Am I interrupting something here?"

Claudia and Hayden both turned to greet their granddaughter, but not before they'd exchanged a look that said they'd take the kiss up again once all their guests departed.

"Not at all," Hayden assured her.

"Mom says you wanted to see me."

Gayla's dark hair and blue eyes resembled her grandfather's while her soft features favored Claudia. And in her, the couple saw themselves as they had been fifty years ago when the opal had first brought them together.

"That's right," Claudia told her. "We have something to give you."

Hayden pulled the velvet box from the pocket of his shirt and handed it his granddaughter.

"And we've been waiting for twenty-one years for this moment," Hayden added.

She giggled. "Well, I can't imagine why you had to wait so long. I've had twenty other birthdays besides this one." Gayla flipped open the box, then stared in surprise at the opal ring gazing up at her. "Oh, a ring."

Claudia and Hayden moved closer as they both carefully watched their granddaughter's reaction.

"It's not just a ring, Gayla," Claudia told her, repeating the same words she'd heard from Betty Fay so many years ago. "It's a special ring."

Gayla looked up at her grandparents as though she was worried about approaching dementia. "What do you mean by 'special'? It looks old to me."

"It is old," Hayden told her. "Your great-great-grandfather got it over in Europe from an old Gypsy woman back during World War II. The ring is blessed and has absorbed the power of everlasting love."

"And when you wear it, the ring will lead you to your one true love," Claudia added.

Unconvinced, but clearly pleased with the ring itself, Gayla slipped the opal onto her finger, then held her hand up to admire the stone. "How could you know such a thing, Gran? The whole thing sounds like a far-out story to me."

Laughing, Claudia looked up at her beloved husband. "That's the same thing your grandfather said to me fifty years ago. But now we believe in stories and in rainbows. And in love."

* * * * *

Silhouette Books is proud to present:

Going to the Chapel

**Three brand-new stories
about getting that special man to the altar!**

featuring

USA Today bestselling author

SHARON SALA

It Happened One Night...that Georgia society belle
Harley June Beaumont went to Vegas—and woke up married!
How could she explain her hunk of a husband to
her family back home?

Award-winning author

DIXIE BROWNING

Marrying a Millionaire...was exactly what Grace McCall was
trying to keep her baby sister from doing. Not that Grace had
anything against the groom—it was the groom's arrogant
millionaire uncle who got Grace all hot and bothered!

National bestselling author

STELLA BAGWELL

The Bride's Big Adventure...was escaping her handpicked
fiancé in the arms of a hot-blooded cowboy! And from the
moment Gloria Rhodes said "I do" to her rugged groom, she
dreamed their wedded bliss would never end!

Available in July at your favorite retail outlets!

Silhouette®

Where love comes alive™

Visit Silhouette at www.eHarlequin.com   PSGTCC

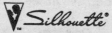

Start Your Summer With Sizzle
And Silhouette Books!

In June 2002, look for these HOT volumes led by *New York Times* bestselling authors and receive a free Gourmet Garden kit!

Retail value of $17.00 U.S.

THE BLUEST EYES IN TEXAS by Joan Johnston
and WIFE IN NAME ONLY by Carolyn Zane

THE LEOPARD'S WOMAN by Linda Lael Miller
and WHITE WOLF by Lindsay McKenna

THE BOUNTY by Rebecca Brandewyne
and A LITTLE TEXAS TWO-STEP by Peggy Moreland

OVERLOAD by Linda Howard
and IF A MAN ANSWERS by Merline Lovelace

This exciting promotion is available at your favorite retail outlet. See inside books for details.

Only from

Silhouette®

TM *Where love comes alive*™

Visit Silhouette at www.eHarlequin.com

PSNCP02

You've shared love, tears and laughter.

Now share your love of reading—

give your daughter Silhouette Romance® novels.

Silhouette®
Where love comes alive™

ANN MAJOR
CHRISTINE RIMMER
BEVERLY BARTON

cordially invite you to attend the year's most exclusive party at the **LONE STAR COUNTRY CLUB!**

Meet three very different young women who'll discover that wishes *can* come true!

LONE STAR
COUNTRY CLUB:
The Debutantes

**Lone Star Country Club:
Where Texas society reigns
supreme—and appearances
are *everything*.**

Available in May
at your favorite retail outlet,
only from Silhouette.

Silhouette®
Where love comes alive™

PSLSCCTD

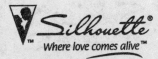